REFUGE

REFUGE

SARDIS PRESS
Box 11 Cascade CO 80809
Published in association with
Liberty House Publishers
Box 10307 Lynchburg VA 24506
printed in the United States of America

1   3   5   7   9   10 8   6   4   2

cover & interior design by
Lee Fredrickson & associates

LIBRARY CATALOGING-IN-PUBLICATION DATA AS FOLLOWS

Olsen, Mark
Refuge/Mark Olsen-1st edition
p.   cm.
ISBN 0-9639465-2-8
Includes afterward and appendix of quotations
1. Parental rights—Fiction.   2. Gay rights—Political—Fiction.
3. Amendment 2—Colorado—Fiction.
4. Religious Right—Fiction
I. Title.
1996

REFUGE

SARDIS PRESS
Box 11
Cascade, CO 80809

**"I will look to the mountains;
from whence shall my help come?"**
– Psalm 121: 1-2 (NASB)

IMPORTANT NOTE:
The quotes and events preceding
each chapter are factual, accurate,
and documented in an appendix
at the end of the book.

Acknowledgements

I owe a huge debt of gratitude to three gifted writers who gave of themselves to this book. First, to Stephen Bransford, without whose enthusiasm, experience and unshakable integrity *Refuge* simply would not have happened. Stephen, thank you for your unending generosity. And to the gifted Bob Liparulo, who gave freely of his freewill editing, marketing wizardry and warm friendship. Mark W. brought keen insight and a compassion for the characters which had a pivotal influence on shaping this story. Special thanks also to Becky Johnson for first-rate editing. Thank you all.

I also thank my friends at Colorado for Family Values: Will Perkins and the board, Jim Witmer, Kevin Tebedo and Tony Marco. Thank you for your open-mindedness in welcoming a bohemian writer into your midst. It's been an honor working with you all.

Personally, I want to thank my parents, Walther and Rachel Olsen, who —living rebuttals to all the cliches about Baptist pastors — always encouraged my creativity, nurtured my free-thinking ways, and modeled for me their own passion for the arts. Finally, last and yet foremost, I want to thank my beloved Connie, my lifelong companion, most fervent supporter, wife, and best friend.

1992. *Colorado voters pass Amendment 2, a state constitutional initiative barring minority privileges based on "sexual orientation." A legal challenge is filed.*

1996. *The United States Supreme Court rules Amendment 2 "unconstitutional," declaring by a 6-3 vote that any "independently identifiable" group of Americans has a constitutional right to not be adversely affected by the outcome of a democratic vote.*

1996. *Gay rights activist rabbi Stephen Foster tells a cheering crowd of thousands outside the State Capitol, "This is not a time to extend the arm of friendship! This is a war and it has not been won!"*

1997. *Gay activists push through a statewide "gay rights" bill in Colorado, making it a crime for someone who disapproves of homosexuality to exercise their freedom of association.*

1997. *Activists pass a revised "hate crimes" bill making it illegal to speak negatively about homosexuality.*

1997. *State educational authorities approve new curricula including pro-homosexual "sensitivity training," "multicultural awareness," and teaching about the "diversity of sexual orientations."*

**And now, a year
in the very near future ...**

... now the tide has turned. We have at last 'come out,' and in doing so have exposed the mean-spirited nature of Judeo-Christian morality ... But with the help of a growing number of your own membership, we are going to force you to recant everything you have believed or said about sexuality ... we will subject Orthodox Jews and Christians to the most sustained hatred and vilification in recent memory. We have captured the liberal establishment and the press. We have already beaten you on a number of battlefields. And we have the spirit of the age on our side. You have neither the faith nor the strength to fight us, so you might as well surrender now."

Gay activist Steve Warren
writing in *The Advocate*, 1987.

ONE

"**M**ommy, tell me a story."

"Which one, Precious?"

"The story about what used to be. About when we used to go on church picnics and play with our friends, and we didn't have to look out for Agents. And nobody wanted to put Pastor Jim in jail."

"Honey, maybe some other time."

"Please? And about when the church was still open, and all the children played out in the field and they didn't even wonder if the police were gonna come and get 'em."

"Heather, Mommy doesn't feel like it right now."

"Please tell it to me. Cause I'm starting to forget. I can't remember those days anymore. Mommy are you ... are you...? Please don't cry, Mommy. Mommies aren't supposed to do that."

Years from now he will remember every detail of the moment his life exploded around him.

He will remember harsh kitchen glare, the cola can upon the counter and the chill of the open freezer, ice cubes rattling like bones in the plastic mug, when from nowhere

John slams into him, smelling of dirt and playground sweat, clamps his nine-year old arms around his father's waist, his high child's voice breathlessly unraveling a tale of policemen with endless questions, of running and running from the pursuit of a drab green car. He will remember how the subtle timbre of truth in his son's voice causes him to step into the living room and see that very car framed in the window, that government car, looming dark and menacing at the curb, and the blood draining from his face as though fleeing the thoughts that flood his mind: *why us ... why today ... what line did we cross ... what did we do to trigger this ... who said the wrong thing to the wrong person ... did someone turn us in ...*

Then his thoughts crash and the world turns silent, and he feels nothing now but panic, the weight of Johnny in his arms, a wild lunge into the garage to heave the boy into the old pickup's cab, and then, seconds later, the startled growl of the old pickup's engine underfoot, the fumes assailing him as the garage door opens too slowly, then splinters around them as he crashes through ...

He will never forget leaving his home forever — the screech of his tires on the driveway, or, backing out, the crunch of the green car's bumper into his own, or the white-shirted figure of the Social Services agent racing back across his lawn from the front door.

It all happens at a strange speed, as though underwater. By the time he returns to himself, the noontime traffic of Baseline Drive is weaving wildly past his windshield. He will remember feeling suddenly overwhelmed by a craving for shelter, up there among the green forests filling his horizon.

The mountains.

And he will remember the sirens. He will never forget the sound of them, howling across a thousand rooftops, just for him.

◆ ◆ ◆

Police search for fugitive parent, son

News Services

BOULDER COUNTY–Child protection and hate-crimes authorities called off their search Monday for fugitive activist Vernon Yates and captive son John, 9. Armed with multiple child abuse counts ranging from homophobic indoctrination to kidnapping of an atonomous minor, authorities vow to keep a nationwide alert for his capture.

Police found Yates' abandoned pickup truck outside of nearby Nederland, where a store owner reported selling a large assortment of foods and backpacking equipment to the pair. "We believe he's taken the boy to where the fugitive networks operate," reports Special Agent James Gruner, "high up in the Rockies."

A campfire blooms in the night, a flicker against the vast slope of a mountain pass.

Vern stands before the flames, reaches out and kneads the warmth with numb fingers. Three feet away his son's stricken face stares across the dancing light. The small red hands rub together, imitating.

The boy's eyes sweep over his face like the inquisitive brush of a hand. *He must be starving for even the smallest sign of reassurance,* Vern tells himself. If only, for just a second, he could answer the questions burning through those young features.

The fear is like a searing band around his chest, drawn to breaking. Every scurry, every rustle in the trees sounds an alarm. Each quiver of firelight snaps his head rigid, his eyes frozen. He feels he cannot breathe. If only for the strength to step around, pick the boy up and squeeze the fear from that small shivering body. Yet some bitter inertia holds him back. He holds his hands toward the flames and forces his weak smile to convey the warmth his body will not let him give.

His eyes roam upwards, but the star-flooded night offers no peace. He pictures helicopters up there plying the dark skies, searching — training nightvision scopes and infrared goggles across the peaks. His gaze drifts downwards, toward the valley, and his mind follows the trail through its center which leads to roads which empty into towns and eventually into cities, and in those cities, officers speaking curtly into radios and cellular phones, working frantically to prosecute this crime he has committed.

He grows slowly aware, emerging from the roar of adrenaline, that he and his son stand in a sublime place. The mountain sleeps here in a deep peace, its silence broken only by a night wind flowing through spruce branches above them. A glow just beyond the granite ridge overhead signals a coming moonrise. From the valley far below drifts the soft gurgle of a stream.

He wishes he could run some more. Run beyond endurance, to a refuge so remote and pristine the government would never dream of its existence.

Only ... not without his family restored. Not without Gail. Not without their youngest, four-year-old Heather, whose enormous blue eyes afflict his thoughts. *How could I have been so stupid? So afraid?* Unable to bear the inner accusations, his mind returns to the sound of his son's voice.

"It was my fault, wasn't it, Dad?"

"No, John. It wasn't."

"If I hadn't told them my name or talked to 'em, it wouldn't have happened. We'd all be together; Mom, Heather ..."

"Son, you did nothing wrong."

"They didn't look like strangers to be afraid of. They said they'd give me a ride home. And then in the car, they started asking these questions."

Vern nods, feeling the weight pull harder at the pit of his stomach.

"They asked me if my mom and dad homeschooled me. They asked me what my mom and dad taught me about gay people. I told them we believe it's a sickness that makes some people do things God doesn't want them to."

"You told them right."

"But then they told me it was wrong to hate people."
The boy pauses, his brows furrowing deeply. "Was it
really hate, Dad, what I said?"

"No, son. It's not hate to say that God doesn't approve
of something a person does. Hate is something like telling somebody that God doesn't love them, or doesn't want
them in the world. Or telling someone that you wish they
had never been born. Wishing they were dead."

"You'd spank me if I said those things about somebody."
John's eyes plead for an answer. "So why did they say I
hated people, when it wasn't true?"

Vern takes a deep breath. He shakes his head for a long
moment, staring into the fire. "Johnny, do you remember
the other day, when we all went out to the mall together,
and Heather wanted some ice cream?"

"Yeah ..."

"And do you remember how she acted when Mom and
Dad told her she couldn't have any?"

"Yeah. She started jumping up and down and crying
and screaming real loud. And everybody looked at us."

"Right. And do you remember what she said?"

"She ... she said you and Mom didn't love her."

"Exactly. And of course we all know that's silly. We
love her very much. It's just that we disagreed with her.
We didn't think it would be good for her stomach to have
ice cream right before supper. Little children sometimes
say things like that when they don't get their way."

Vern leans back and drops another branch on the fire,
spewing a blaze of sparks into the air. "Some grown-ups
act that way too, sometimes. Especially some of the grown-
ups who call themselves gay."

"Are those ..." John hesitates, his eyes suddenly anxious, "are those the people at the church that one time?"

Vern nods slowly. He moves over beside his son and
hugs him in a tight embrace. He had hoped his son would
forget the trauma of that day.

The family unit — spawning ground of lies, betrayals, mediocrity, hypocrisy and violence — will be abolished.

The family unit, which only dampens imagination and curbs free will, must be eliminated.

Gay activist Michael Swift writing in "Towards a Homoerotic Order," 1987.

TWO

A bright, blue Sunday.

One year ago.

Late for evening service, Vern steers the van onto Baseline Road and immediately notices, down at the end of the block, that things in front of the church don't look normal. A thick mass of people, milling about. Police cars. Movement, frenzied and chaotic. Painted rainbows and pink triangles bob above the surging crowd.

He senses Gail's anxious face turned toward his, but he does not acknowledge her alarm. "Vern," she calls anxiously, "shouldn't we turn around and go home?"

"No! I'm not going to let these people keep me from my own church. It's our parking lot. I'm going to drive onto it and they can just try and get in my way."

A chant pierces through the clamor, loud and angry. "Shame! Shame! All this hate in Jesus' name!" He allows himself to consider their slogan, for the briefest of seconds — these radicals who accuse his wife and children of hate even while they terrorize them in front of their own church. Where's the hate right now? In the terrified faces of his innocent family, or the snarls of these rioters?

Vern's eyes meet those of an emaciated man with orange-dyed butch-cut hair, blowing through a whistle with more venom than his fragile body seems capable of. Vern squints through the windshield at him, as if a deeper look will discern some glowing ember of humanity. Instead he sees only flat, animal rage. Mindless fury. Out of fear as much as anger, he pushes into the center of the steering wheel and the horn rings out into the crowd.

His foot presses on the accelerator. It feels good, the thought of ramming it to the floor, clearing a swath through these people. But no. That way lies madness. He nudges forward slowly.

The van surges through a clearing in the mob and into a parking space, the shouting right behind them. As their engine shuts off, the mob engulfs them. Angry faces darken the windows, glaring in. Grasping the wheel hard, he sees flashes of pink halter tops, tanned and muscular arms shaking fists towards him and his family. Then the pounding begins. His ears fill with the loud thumping of fists on windows, then Heather's voice rising in a thin wail, and soon John's. Finally even Gail screams beside him as the glass begins to shudder beneath thundering blows. The shrieks from outside grow almost as loud as those from within.

Then suddenly two friendly faces appear in Gail's window: Dave Dixon and Mel Barrows, church deacons. The two are also ex-college football players, he remembers at the sight of their broad shoulders and grim, determined expressions. Huddling against the van on Vern's side, Dave motions sideways with his head. *Come on. We'll shield you.*

Vern cracks the door and the clamor rushes in, deafening now. He lurches across the van's shallow hood while the men evacuate Gail and the children and prepare a sort of flying wedge before them, facing the crowd.

Vern looks around quickly. Atop the church flagpole, where the American and Christian flags usually fly, now

waves a rainbow flag. Gay pride. Where in the world are
the police? He saw patrol cars — where are the officers?
Scanning, he spots two of them standing in the road,
watching. Hands on their hips. Their eyes sweep the
crowd, but their body language betrays their impotence.
Why aren't there dozens of officers? And paddywagons?
Shaking his head in anger, Vern picks screaming Heather
up into his arms and cradles her head in his shoulder,
desperately wishing he could drown out the noise.

"Let's go!"

With a gritting of teeth and a tensing of muscles, they're
off, the men's feet shuffling, the small group moving forward into the crowd. The bedlam grows even louder, as if
the rioters are provoked by their movement. Fists rain
down on Vern's arms and back, but he cannot let Heather
go; he can only crouch lower and keep moving. Another
scream rings out above the others and he recognizes Gail's
voice — he turns to see her white-sweatered body being
jerked away ... *No, this is impossible, this can't be happening* ... her body is rising, the rioters carrying her off
the ground and into their midst. What can he do? Holding his daughter he is torn for a second, then he sees Dave,
thank God, disengage and go into an old linebacker's
crouch, barreling through bodies towards her. With a
lunging shoulder he knocks down two rioters in his way,
then leans forward and catches Gail's hands. He pulls
hard and she breaks free from the rioters' grasp, tum-
bling towards him.

They climb steps and the rioters fall away, almost as if
repelled by the church doors. Eager faces surrounding
the entrance grow closer. Then, in a flurry, they're inside.
People surround them offering hugs and blankets, but
despite the reception, his children cannot stop crying. The
muted lighting and thick carpets that always seemed
soothingly appropriate for a church interior now clash
with the anguish of the people milling about, dazed and
weeping. Through a glass wall he can see Pastor Miller

in the church office, speaking urgently into a telephone.

"Captain, they've taken over the church grounds. Total control. They've not only terrorized my congregation, but they've turned over the fountain, destroyed the landscaping, torn down the flag ... They're pounding on the doors right now! Listen for yourself!"

Eyes blazing, the pastor yanks the phone cord away and punches a fist into the lobby, holding the phone towards the entrance. A deep pounding fills the corridor as the doors buckle from ramming blows. A metallic, amplified voice shouts, "We want your children!"

At once the image sears into Vern's memory: Johnny's small back silhouetted against the window and the furious mob framed beyond it, where, atop another's shoulders, sits a man holding a megaphone, his eyes trained fiercely upon his son.

"WE WANT YOUR CHILDREN! WE WANT YOUR CHILDREN!"

Johnny turns at the sound of his father's approach, tears already pouring from his eyes. As Vern gathers him up the boy convulses furiously, his entire upper body engulfed by sobs. "They want me! They want me! It's me they want!" Vern holds his son until his arms give out. They sink to the floor.

They are still there fifteen minutes later, a father speaking soft comforting words into his son's ear, when the dark forms of the riot police trucks arrive.

And then, the crowning insult. The morning Boulder newspaper.

Police break up pro-tolerance demonstration
A Boulder Daily Telegraph editorial

BOULDER–A lively pro-tolerance demonstration by a band of spirited local activists was broken up with riot squads last Sunday before evening services at Boulder's homophobic Second Baptist Church.

Predictably, the First Amendment came to a screeching halt as fundamentalist Pastor John Miller called armed squads against a group whose only crime was expressing their passion for civil rights.

It has now become a typical pattern: right-wing extremists like Pastor Miller assume that the only response to a diverse view is the blunt end of a billy club. The question is, what is the Radical Right so afraid of? Why do they feel it necessary to call out the troops at the first sight of a dissenting opinion? Wouldn't it be nice if the bigots would try the path of dialogue once in a while?

Perhaps most galling of all is that after squelching the free speech of gay-rights activists, these fundamentalists go on to whine piously about the supposed erosion of their freedom of religion.

Please. We all know who has eroded civil rights and inflicted untold misery on America's minorities all these years. That's right. The Christian God and the whole cult of Judeo-Christian so-called thought, which for so long held our nation in its iron grip.

Surely, the freedom of religion established by our Founding Fathers did not include the right to persevere in such obvious fallacies as the Bible's outmoded approach to sexuality. Constitutional rights are for real Americans. The only thing these extremists have in common with the rest of America is citizenship and an accident of geography.

So next time you drive by the Second Baptist Church — especially between eleven o'clock and noon on Sunday mornings — give a good, long honk for the First Amendment.

Boy lovers and the lesbians who have young lovers ... are not child molesters. The child abusers are priests, teachers, therapists, cops and parents who force their staid morality onto the young people in their custody.

Lesbian author Pat Califia, 1981.

THREE

Now, sitting on a fallen pine limb in the darkened wilderness, the memory of that day seems almost quaint. Such a distant time, when he could still be surprised at the thought of being considered an enemy, a bigot. Part of the problem. Today, just over a year later, the establishment's implacable hostility seems a fact of life, like the color of the sky.

"Yes, John. Those people in front of the church were some of the people who call themselves gay, and who say we hate them."

"Why do they act that way?"

He lets out a weary puff at that one. How can he answer, without pulling down the whole sorry catalog of twentieth century sexuality down into his son's young mind?

"Well ... we believe they're people who are wounded in their spirits, so that when they grow up, instead of falling in love with a woman like God intended, they fall in love with other men. Or women with women. And their wounded spirits make them believe it's normal and not only that, but makes them get really, really mad at anybody who doesn't agree with them."

"So that's why they say we hate them when actually we don't."

"Yes. They're wrong. Sometimes grown-ups can be very, very wrong. They threw a fit that Sunday and when they couldn't change our minds, they threw more fits in front of folks like judges and school principals and the people in Congress, screaming that we hated them, screaming that someone should make it against the law to disagree with them. And after they screamed long enough, these folks gave them what they wanted."

"So the good guys are against us?"

"What do you mean, 'good guys'?"

"You know — on TV the good guys and the policemen always protect the other people getting picked on, and stand up for truth and stuff."

"Right. In real life the good guys are mistaken too. Somebody told them a lie and they believed it. So they're on the wrong side right now. But maybe pretty soon they'll realize it and start being the good guys again."

"But we don't hate them for it."

Something about John's voice just then, its guileless blend of curiosity and innocence, compels Vern to turn and look at the boy, and the purity of his son's gaze engulfs him. Without warning, Vern finds himself struggling with all his might to calm his heaving lungs. He cannot; even as he tries to suppress the sobs they surge from his gut and engulf his chest in a wrenching series of convulsions. He cannot cry. He must not cry. His voice escapes with a strange wordless cry as he strains to silence himself. He looks away to the forest and wills himself to breathe. Just breathe. He feels someone touch him and then two arms encircle his neck and shoulder. He turns slightly to his son's face pressed hard against an arm, the boy's expression cycling between terror and a calm, determined sort of pity.

The son holds the father for several long moments. Slowly Vern feels calm return. He lets the mountain's peace sweep over him, then takes a long breath. Restored to the comfortable boundaries of fatherhood, Vern hugs his son tightly, then hands him his sleeping bag. "Get some rest. They'll probably be back after us early in the morning."

The boy sits and pulls the flannel lining over his matted brown hair.

Through firelight Vern studies the edges of the clearing, this remote place where he has brought his son. He turns to the fire. Feeding it enough to keep the boy warm will keep him awake through the night. Just as well, for his anger and frustration will surely fuel him well past daybreak. He reaches into his knapsack for a pen and frayed legal pad and begins to write.

> *Dear Gail,*
>   *If only I could tell you how broken I feel without you here.*
>   *I'm sure you're wondering why I ran. Why I took John and left without you and Heather. Did I do it out of cowardice, did I think of you, did I just let panic get the best of me ...*
>   *I'm so sorry you're having to sort through these questions alone. Truth is, it was either run or get arrested. The Social Services car was already parked in front of the house when I took off. I chose to run, and there was no time to find you. I knew you and Heather were out shopping somewhere, but I had no idea where. I heard the sirens following me and I just panicked.*
>   *It was bound to happen eventually, I guess. I only wish we'd been more prepared. In hindsight I think we were foolish not to have been ready. With all the laws being passed against us, the extra patrols, all the stories we've been hearing. I hold myself to blame. I just thought we had more time to get ready to become fugitives.*
>   *What happened was this. John was walking*

from the park when some agents pulled up, gave him ride, started asking him questions. Same old story. Only now it's our family the victim, instead of some poor slob we just hear about.

Gail, you'd be so proud of our son. Unfortunately, he realizes everything that's happened. The injustice of it. The hypocrisy. He's bearing up really well. It all happened so fast. I was at home getting a drink when Johnny busted in. I didn't think — I just reacted. Thank God the camping equipment was already in the back of the truck. I just grabbed him, practically threw him in, and took off. There wasn't time to think, Darling.

I don't know what to do. I'm going to try and hook up with the Refuge somehow. All I know is to keep on, keep resisting and keep praying for a way to get our family back together. And keep the faith. I don't know how we're going to get through this, but I promise I'll find a way. As long as John and I are free, at least our family has a fighting chance.

Please forgive me for leaving you behind. There just wasn't time.

I love you.

Vern.

He holds the paper and reads it through a few times. He breathes carefully, deeply. No, he will not give in to tears again. He would never stop. Slowly, it occurs to him that he cannot send this letter. Gail's mail is surely being monitored. Inside, he winds himself up a notch tighter, takes one more look, then drops it into the flames.

John's light snore tells him that at least one of them will sleep tonight. He stows the writing gear in the pack and sits awhile, watching the dying fire, wondering what he'd been thinking, bringing children into a world where families have become outlaws, where faith goes under the name of hatred, and discernment goes under the name of insanity ...

Homophobia officially named mental disorder

News Services

SAN FRANCISCO — At its annual convention last week, the American Psychological Association added homophobia to the fifth edition of its Diagnostic and Statistical Manual of Disorders, or DSM-5, widely considered to be the nation's official register of mental illnesses.

Ratified by a majority of the Association's membership, the move capped a decade-long effort by gay and lesbian mental health professionals to recognize what they call the "pathology of hatred."

The designation, which carries far-reaching social and legal consequences to those afflicted with the disorder, was criticized by Christian fundamentalists and the religious right in general. They claim the term "homophobia" has been diluted to include even principled disagreement with gay viewpoints.

But gay activists are quick to place opposition in perspective. "The radical right has always opposed advances in mental health," says expert Robert Millman, "especially now that such progress exposes the truly deranged aspect of their fundamental beliefs."

Soon, far too soon, Vern opens his eyes to the glare of daylight and the sight of his son's face looming over him, outstretched arms shaking him gently. He scrambles to his feet without a word. Silently, both gather their belongings and stuff them into packs. Finally, with a deep loud sigh and a slap on the boy's shoulders, he turns towards the mountain.

The two figures recede quickly into the wilderness, and vanish.

Three hours and twenty minutes later, the sun high now in the sky, a lone hiker comes slowly upon the campsite.

The stocky frame fills brown camouflage fatigues; the feet, black army boots caked with dust. With a heavy grunt a trail pack comes crashing to the ground. The hand runs through spiky blond hair, pulls away black, small-round sunglasses, rips a lavender bandana loose from a sunburned throat.

She has been hiking for three hours already, since before dawn. Turning, she crouches intently over the ashes of a small firepit. She turns the ashes in her fingers, feeling the warmth. She looks away to the tracks in the soft ground. Fresh. One large man, one smaller individual. A child, probably.

A long, deep chuckle escapes from her. Amazing how stupid these Christians can be. Sonya, butch lesbian, deputized tracker for the Colorado State Patrol, has finally, as usual, picked up the trail.

She stands, looks at her watch. She makes a bet with herself — she'll have the collar made by late afternoon. With a young boy in tow, the homophobe is no match. She almost wishes it could be a more evenly matched contest. She toys with the idea of following procedure, radioing in for a unit to pick them up at the end of the trail. No way. She'll keep this one for herself. She wants the pleasure of handcuffing this bigot with his little boy sitting there, watching. And then, the pleasure of turning to the kid and muttering, in a low voice, "Son, this man has been teaching you something sick and illegal. And he's never going to do it again."

At the very second the pack is swinging over her shoulder again, the pager sounds an annoying beep. How strange, she thinks, to hear such a noise on a wild mountainside like this. She picks up the small black case from her waist and checks the display. All nines — emergency. She curses softly. Somebody must have beat her to it, found them already. Betraying every urge in her body, she turns away from the still-warm trail and heads back toward her truck.

By the time she pulls in beside the patrol car at the highway crossing in Nederland, a small, funky town just up the road from Boulder, her frustration has simmered into a low, sullen anger. The trooper looks up at her, his face slack with professional apathy. "Man and a boy spotted down at Boulder Falls with big packs on. This eyewitness said they looked real nervous."

"When?"

"First thing this morning."

"Which way'd they go?"

He turns from the window to check his notepad, then reappears. "The lady said they headed down. East."

Doesn't sound right. "What's the description?"

"She said the man was in his late thirties, five-ten, 180 pounds, light brown hair, full beard, and the boy ..."

"And a *beard?*" A string of obscenities pours loudly from her. "You idiot! Vern Yates doesn't have a beard!"

"You don't know that. He hasn't shaved in a couple days. He could have put on a disguise."

"I doubt it. Besides, they're not headed east — that's where they came from! They're a good twenty miles west of Boulder Falls. And I was closing in on them! Until your stupid call came in, that is. I would have had 'em by now!"

With a stony look he jerks his gearshift back into drive. She returns the glare. He knows he screwed up, but she reminds herself that no matter how wrong they are, state troopers hate to be told. They hate trackers like her, period. Tough, she tells herself as his car speeds away. This mistake just cost her the collar of the year.

By now, the two could be anywhere.

He went and filed a complaint with the city. Three days later the police showed up, took me in to the police station. At first I couldn't believe it. I mean, isn't there something called freedom of association? Aren't we supposed to be able to choose the people we live with and hang out with, in this country?

— A refugee

All churches who oppose us will be closed.
Our only gods are handsome young men ...

Michael Swift, "Towards a Homoerotic Order," 1987.

The rioters assumed complete control of the
exterior property and grounds of the church.... . The
guest speaker was escorted by police to the church as
debris from the rioters pelted him from all sides.... .
When the rioters saw children standing in the lobby,
they shouted, 'We want your children! Give us your
children!' ... A nine-year-old boy was crying in hys-
terics. 'They are after me. It's me they want.' He did
not calm down until the family was several miles
from the building.

Excerpts from the report of Pastor David Innes
of Hamilton Square Baptist Church, San Francisco,
following a 1993 mob attack by several hundred gay
activists.

FOUR

Two days later, a truck hauling groceries to Estes Park rounds a turn on what is known as the Peak to Peak Highway, a road snaking north along the northwestern edge of the Front Range. Negotiating the turn at sixty miles an hour, the driver does not notice two backpackers hurrying across the road behind him.

A man in his late thirties, a young boy.

They run across the pavement faster than mere highway caution would dictate, their packs lurching awkwardly behind them. Instead of following the ditch to a nearby trailhead, they dart straight into the trees and disappear.

They have been visible, there atop the highway, for a total of twenty seconds.

As they leave the highway behind and recede further into the wilderness, Vern finds that their surroundings help him forget his troubles for brief, blessed moments. The beauty of the mountains wraps him in a mood of quiet, endless calm. The boy seems to feel it too; the frenetic tension of the first few days has left his face. He looks about him more, drinking in the cool, piney air, the sight of trees and distant summits. It occurs to Vern that this is the first time he has backpacked with his son. Actually, this is the longest stretch of time he has ever spent alone with the boy. What a way to start. He wonders, if all this hadn't happened, would he have ever found the time to take him into the mountains?

They climb quickly, silently through a thick, old forest, green with the new growth of spring. A stronger whiff of pine drifts across their path, taking Vern back to summer camp, an eternity ago. A time when his adult life stretched far before him like a placid, untroubled river — no complications worth worrying over beyond surviving college and marrying a beautiful girl. Even politics had seemed an irrelevant abstraction. He'd barely even heard of homosexuality, let alone gay militancy.

In fact, it was years after first hearing those names float across the playgrounds of his youth, that he knew what they meant.

Fag. Queer. Homo.

His buddies had started using them in junior high school, words of unknown meaning, devoid of literal content yet somehow charged with psychic firepower. He soon learned the shocking truth — that some guys were more attracted to other guys than to immaculate blond cheerleaders with clingy jeans and soft, inviting eyes. It made him shudder, the first time he heard of it. *Gross.*

When his high school buddies had started proposing trips out to the nearest gay bar for quick rounds of "fag bashing," Vern had always declined. No matter how alien the concept of homosexuality, he had always felt the wrongness of attacking these people, even then.

He remembers that friend from junior college days. Ray. The best programmer in the class, and in his spare time a talented singer in a local garage band. Vern remembers a lanky frame and sharp blue eyes, full of intelligence and an untouchable air of sadness. He often believed he could see enormous currents of pain in Ray's eyes, suffering that seemed the result of deep, unyielding bondage.

Studying for their finals one day, Vern had asked and

Ray had finally admitted it, eyes refusing to meet his. Thereafter the subject would come up from time to time, after class, out on campus. Ray was no activist. He took no inordinate pride in the fact, wasn't adamant about how great it was. It was just something he felt unable to change. Vern had eventually conveyed his own position on the issue, softly, almost reluctantly — that he didn't agree with the life-style, but that didn't mean he didn't consider Ray a good friend or a worthwhile person. It just meant he had his own feelings on the matter.

Vern realizes, thinking back, that Ray had accepted their amicable stalemate. The guy had never had a problem distinguishing between disapproval of homosexuality and hatred. After graduation Ray had faded off into the obscurity of the working world, but years later, when gay rights had flared into the cultural flash point of the decade, Vern had wondered about him.

These days he finds himself scanning pictures of gay mobs for the familiar outline of Ray's face, hoping not to find it, relieved each time he does not. *Has Ray become one of them too, blowing whistles and raising fists? Please, no. But where did they go, the everyday gays and lesbians like him, who aren't driven to push their life-style down everybody's throat? Where are the Rays of the gay movement?*

Still pursued by the thought of that highway so close behind, Vern pushes their pace up the mountainside, trying to quickly increase the distance between them and civilization. Time moves slowly, with the patient laboring of lungs and the methodical plodding of feet.

After a half mile they emerge onto a high ridgeline and pause before a magnificent sight. A wide valley stretches away towards the West, tracking a distinct Y shape around a high mountain swathed in forests. Along the valley's thick green floor lies a series of blue lakes, their clear surfaces sparkling in the sun. Catching his breath, John straightens up and squints, looking out.

"That's the Continental Divide, there at the top," Vern tells him.

"Are we gonna cross it?"

"Yeah. We sure are."

The wrenching desperation of their flight suddenly returns. He should be pointing out this kind of beauty on a casual weekend hike with his son. Not running for his family's survival.

How did the years ahead of me used to look, back when they seemed clearer and straighter than a hundred miles of Kansas highway?

Live here in Boulder. Raise two well-adjusted kids. Work hard. Get to know God a whole lot better. Serve Him the best we could, and stay active in church. Maybe someday I'd have hatched some hot software idea and started a business out of the house — at least get to stay home with the kids more. Maybe even get lucky with it and gain the freedom to travel more, worry less.

The years would go by slow and happy. Then one day Gail and I would look around and realize the kids had grown up and the careers had run their course. Retirement would give us the time to become serious tourists. Things would slow down. Life would blossom into a big golden sunset punctuated by holidays, grandchildren and vacations.

That's all. Didn't seem like outrageous expectations at the time. Didn't seem such an ambitious life that I'd have get into this mess just trying to protect it. One thing's for sure: my life wasn't supposed to hinge on some detour like gay rights — pro or con. I never wanted to become some fiery activist, or let myself get all worked up over some political issue. Most of my life, I was never into politics at all.

No, I didn't choose it. It was forced on me. I never had any beef with gays until they started poking their noses into how I lived my life — raised my kids, ran my business. What was I to do — when I couldn't send my kids to school without having them indoctrinated in something I opposed with every bone in my body? Or when I couldn't go to work without being ordered to betray my beliefs? When I couldn't go to church without the need for bodyguards? When I could be labeled "insane" and lose my kids just for teaching them the Bible?

Now, I don't think about the future. I think about today. Covering some ground, evading capture, making it to nightfall with my freedom.

Years later he will describe the slow process of losing his freedom using the words of the old story — the frog who might have jumped from the kettle of suddenly heated water, but was lulled to his death by a gradual flame.

The ultimate irony is that until a few years ago, Vern Yates had never ever thought of himself as a conservative.

Growing up, he had always been cooler than every other Christian kid he knew. In Boulder during the early seventies, he had constantly sported some hip fashion statement or other to set himself apart from the blow-dried world of his childhood faith. Why couldn't everyone understand that Christianity had nothing to do with looking like a tele-vangelist? Or that a guy with long hair and earrings could be just as spiritual as some square, bowl-haired geek who didn't know Led Zeppelin from Lawrence Welk? It frustrated him to no end.

He loved God; he just didn't think it obligated him to be a dork.

In high school he would slip into some of the town's most tie-dyed, bohemian joints with his ponytail and Birkenstocks, sit and drink in the folk songs and the leisurely Celtic jam sessions, silently congratulating himself on the fact that no one around would ever peg him for an evangelical. And then show up at church on Sunday mornings to feel the old ladies eye him suspiciously, wondering how such a hippie-looking boy could possibly be a believer. How could his parents and their kind so smugly alienate the new generation with their conformism and their staid ways? They held their cultural retardation like some kind of badge of purity — he suspected it was really a barrier protecting them from all the undesirables out there smoking dope on the street corners.

In junior college he had discovered computers and his future fell into place. Boulder was full of programming jobs. His colleagues had been stunned, three months into that first job, when the artsy, ponytailed newcomer had casually let it be known that he was of the Christian persuasion. Their surprise had made him feel even more mysterious and unconventional.

By the time the culture wars had raised their ugly heads in the early nineties, he had become a senior programmer and a family man. Gail had turned his life upside down — beginning with a delicious Swedish smile over a church pew one Sunday morning, and then, nine months and two days after their wedding day, with the gift of baby John. And five years later, with beautiful Heather. Life was great. He could live the Boulder life, be a Christian, and not even have to look like one.

By the time he first heard of Amendment 2, the controversial state initiative to limit minority rights based on homosexuality, Vern had seized on his response quicker than most: *paranoid fundamentalists are to blame.* How could people who shared his faith support such a measure? He didn't think homosexuality was a great thing — but couldn't those pinheads come across as loving for once? The issue seemed perfectly simple. Cut and dried. *Rights are good. Rights mean freedom. Any tolerant, compassionate American favors rights — the more, the better. Giving equal rights to all people — even unpopular, unsavory people — is what America is all about. Therefore, anything called "gay rights" has to be a good thing. Conversely, anyone opposing "gay rights" is by definition advocating a rollback of civil liberties, a denial of everything it is to be an American. And what about the separation of Church and State? Christians already have such a bad reputation for trying to impose their morality on the rest of society. Just once, couldn't they get it?*

He publicly condemned the whole thing. Those three vile words began leaving his mouth with the same disgust as everyone else's.

The Religious Right.

When Amendment 2 had passed, he had privately assured all his best friends that "not all Christians are like that." Not all were consumed by paranoia or the need to enforce their agenda on the rest of society. More and more, he felt anger towards those reactionaries; the same slow-burning resentment he had always felt. The beady-eyed Puritanism of his youth had returned to infuriate him. Once again his hip Christian aesthetic was being undermined by the stiff-necked troops of conservatism.

Then Amendment 2 was overturned by the United States Supreme Court. At first he had welcomed the decision. But then he began to read excerpts from the majority opinion. Justice Kennedy hadn't even bothered to rely on legal precedent in writing the decision. The opinion had seemed preachy, opinionated, even shallow — everything a Supreme Court opinion is not supposed to be. Kennedy had blithely stated that only rank animosity could have motivated Amendment 2. For the first time, Vern found himself disagreeing. The arguments had seemed at least subtler than that. He had read Justice Scalia's minority opinion, arguing that homosexuals "… possess political power much greater than their numbers …" and that they "… devote this political power to achieving not merely a grudging social toleration, but full societal acceptance, of homosexuality." He began to discern the ring of truth in Scalia's angry dissent. And he started admitting to himself, quietly, down deep in the pit of his stomach, *Vern, you may have been wrong on this one.*

It had continued with newspaper headlines, crossing his innocent breakfast table, day after day.

"Gays and Lesbians Win Sweeping New Freedoms."

"Public Schools Embrace Rainbow Curriculum."

"Congress Protects Sexual Minorities."

"President Marches at Gay Pride Parade."

A federal law had outlawed discrimination on the basis of sexual orientation nationwide. The face of the Senate Majority Leader had appeared on the evening news, gravely comparing the struggle for gay and lesbian rights with Martin Luther King, Jr.'s struggle for civil rights in the sixties.

Then on TV one night, the President had solemnly announced the stiffening of criminal statutes, all to "give these newfound freedoms the force of law."

Three months later, a sweeping new Hate Crimes bill had showed up in Congress, and how could anyone oppose such a thing? Obviously, anyone against it favored hate — and who wanted "hatemonger" as a label? The bill passed comfortably. The right-wing nuts had complained about its strict hate-speech clauses — provisions making it illegal to speak out against homosexuality — warning that the First Amendment had just been suspended. They were dismissed as agitators. And at first, nothing sinister had happened. All their warnings seemed like so much empty rhetoric.

He had assumed the activists only wanted equal rights, but now...

... now he began to hear stories.

Late one breezy, spring-warm evening, Gail had leaned over in bed and spoken softly about something she'd heard of at school, a father jailed for two and a half months now on some sort of home-schooling violation.

Then at church, they'd heard rumors of pastors being arrested for things they'd been preaching. Most of the evangelical pastors in Colorado had seemingly turned into raving bigots overnight. Menaces to society.

One day, one of these reports had made the newspaper. "Diversity asserts itself," the headline read on the paper's editorial pages. According to the wire services, right-wing America was beginning to reap the whirlwind of its hatred and bigotry towards minorities through the centuries. Fundamentalists were paying a high price for their ways, and it was only going to increase as fairness and pluralism began to assert themselves in America.

Soon the voice was giving him no peace. Days, his mind would churn with incessant fears and doubts about the consequences of his inaction. At night, his sleep became troubled and erratic. Finally, one Saturday morning, Vern had climbed the topmost stairs into his attic and dug an old, caved-in fruit box out of his cellar, filled with old files of Amendment 2 campaign literature. Gail, always more conservative than he, had saved them. He'd picked up brochures at random and spent the next two hours reading.

How had he missed all of it?

Here were direct quotes: homosexual manifestoes advocating the closing of churches, the silencing of political adversaries, the removal of children. Example after example. No mercy for anyone disapproving of homosexuality. Why hadn't anyone warned him? Then he had realized.

He'd never read any of them.

He'd remembered telling himself he was already quite familiar with right-wing rhetoric, and tossed them aside. The warning signs had been there — he'd just been too cool to read them.

Now, he often thinks back to those easy days. Such a simple time, when a ponytail and a pair of faded jeans had meant more to him than the truth.

◆ ◆ ◆

New children's rights bill voids sexual age of consent

News Services

DENVER–State education officials yesterday pledged their full compliance with the just-signed Children's Emancipation Act of 1999. The law, which declares all children "free moral agents and sovereign beings," was passed by Congress last week. In addition to voiding all age-of-consent laws, it subordinates parental privileges to the State's duty to protect children's "ideological autonomy."

That aspect has clearly delighted gay and civil-rights activists. "At last, society is safeguarding children from hazards like the trauma of parental homophobia," activist Nicole Gates pointed out at a noontime news conference. Gates added that, "Protecting our children from parental homophobia in this manner represents a giant leap forward in our nation's commitment to mental health."

God, you've got a lot of explaining to do. Why did you let things sink this far? Is this some sort of punishment? Something I did — something we all did? Something we should have done? All those Sundays sitting in church, I thanked you for the freedom of being an American. And I meant it. Honest.

But did you have to let it all get taken away? If I had some lesson to learn, did you have to go this far to teach me?

I know, God. We were careless. We ignored the signs. But Lord, if we did, we ignored them for the right reasons. We were busy raising our families, going to church, living busy lives. We didn't think this kind of insanity could happen here. How could we imagine all this? All we wanted was to raise our families the way we thought you wanted. What was so outrageous about that, that these people should have to prosecute us? I don't understand. I didn't deserve this ...

1991. *Mandatory "sensitivity training" lectures are held at a state hospital in Pueblo, Colorado. Employees are urged to sign a form acknowledging their "imperfect attitudes toward gays and lesbians" and to wear buttons stating, "it's okay to be gay." Those who decline are walked to the front, told to turn and face their colleagues.*

1994. *George Mason University punishes as "discrimination" the act of "jumping when a homosexual touches you on the arm," and "keeping a physical distance from someone because they are a known gay or lesbian."*

FIVE

They enter the valley and find themselves in the most beautiful alpine world Vern has ever seen. Thick evergreen forests rise abruptly on the flanks of steep, glacier-carved mountains. A stream runs beside their path, its water so clear it is colorless, tinted only from underneath by the rich brown of stones lining its bed. Ahead lies a series of lakes, glittering silver in the sunlight. The smell of mountains rises to them on an afternoon wind — pungent soil, sweet wildflower and fleeting whiffs of evergreen. Vern racks his memory. In all his years he has never heard of such a place this pristine, this untouched.

They walk carefully, slowly, keeping under tree cover. Occasionally the trail breaks into a meadow and they veer away, follow the covering fringe of forest or willow trees.

Suddenly, John freezes. He reaches for his father's pack before him, grabs its pocket and yanks hard. His eyes are huge, fixed. Vern turns and in a frantic second pulls John back behind a nearby boulder.

Less than two hundred yards away stands a teenager speaking into a walkie-talkie, clad in khaki shorts and a light brown windbreaker. His matching cap seems to complete some sort of uniform. The wind carries his voice in barely discernible fragments, "No ... don't ... them ... check ..." He turns, and words upon the back of his jacket come into focus. "City of Boulder."

Now Vern understands. For years he heard rumors of the beautiful, forbidden Boulder watershed, closed to everyone but employees of the city's water department, rigidly patrolled by a team of fanatical young environmentally conscious teenagers. After a time, he had ceased to believe the place really existed. Just another urban myth.

Slowly, the young man moves down the trail, as the pair huddle breathlessly behind their cover. Vern is almost afraid to look at the receding figure, gripped by a sudden fear that the young man will feel himself being watched.

He and John climb deep into the forest, to a small clearing which offers a view of towering peaks overhead. They spend the day there, hidden far from the trail, resting in the sun and speaking in whispers. They do not move out again until nightfall.

The last time I saw my son, I hardly recognized him. The visit was supervised. They warned me not to make any negative statements. Gavin had purple hair and a ring through his nose. And he told us he had a boyfriend.

– A refugee

Several years before, an e-mail message had showed up on Vern's computer screen one day at work. "Sensitivity training — must read." It sounded like an easy break — a morning off work, a few hours spent learning how to get along, how to show sensitivity for colleagues' cultural differences. No problem. Sensitivity had never been a problem for Vern.

Two weeks later he and sixteen other workers had sat in a cool, carpeted conference room as a black woman dressed in rainbow-colored silk robes had stood before them and begun to speak. "Today we are going to learn how to go beyond tolerating each other's differences, and learn to actually value them. We are going to learn how racism, sexism, lookism, and homophobia destroy the working environment, and what we can do to combat these evils."

Vern had looked around him. Seeing only wide, accepting stares, he had felt his stomach sink.

Two hours later, the woman had laid her next transparency on the projector. "Homophobia," read the topic headline, glowing on the wall.

"Let's face the facts," the coordinator began. "If you would gladly attend the funeral of a co-worker's wife, but hesitate to attend that of his gay lover, you suffer from homophobia. If you think sexual orientation is a matter of someone's choice or their environment, you suffer from homophobic thinking. If you privately think less of a colleague after learning he or she is gay or lesbian, you are a homophobe — and the fact is, homophobia destroys working relationships. Furthermore, it's a recognized mental illness, and we're here to help." She smiles maternally. "Now, let's identify specific homophobic thought patterns..."

Vern had felt his legs bearing him upwards. Standing, he felt them lead him towards the door. The instructor spoke, her voice accusing. "Potty break?"

He shook his head. "No. Propaganda break."

"Excuse me?"

"I'm sorry. I hate no one, and I fear no one. But I have beliefs, and my beliefs are being attacked in this seminar."

"Your beliefs include hatred?"

"No, they don't."

He walked out. He turned around, aimed his feet at thedoor, and felt them carry him steadily to his desk. The most exhilarating ninety-second walk of his life.

Two weeks later, he had felt a distinct lack of surprise when his supervisor somberly ushered him into the office and closed the door behind them.

"We don't want to lose you, Vern," the man had said, looking out the window as he spoke. "But the office is in an uproar over your behavior at the Valuing Differences Seminar."

"I just didn't feel it was any of the company's business what lifestyle I endorse with my private actions."

"Well ..." the supervisor began rifling through papers in a folder. "Actually Vern, your employment contract states, 'I will do everything within my power to value the differences between myself and my gay, lesbian, or minority colleagues.' Did you read this before you signed it?"

A grim weight descended on him. "I guess not."

"Vern, it's not an unusual provision. Most large corporations are requiring this these days. Departments of the federal government have been doing it for years."

"Listen," Vern began, his desire to reach the man increasing with the rising timbre of his voice, "I have never treated a gay colleague any different from anyone else. You can ask them that ..."

"Actually, many of them feel uncomfortable with your political views."

"But my views are unspoken! I have never once preached my beliefs around the office!"

"That's not the issue, Vern. Your refusal to affirm their lifestyle creates a hostile working environment for them, and management cannot allow that."

"You're saying it doesn't matter how well I do my job, that because of what I personally believe, beliefs that have nothing to do with the company, nothing to do with the work, that I'm guilty of some sort of on-the-job harassment?"

"I'm not saying that."

"What are you saying, then?"

The man coughed once, then paused, as if a decision

remained to be made. He looked at Vern mournfully, and without looking down, picked up a sheet of paper and handed it to him. Under "reasons for termination" lay the words, "willful failure to appreciate employee morale issues, multicultural awareness, and valuing differences."

The hard-core militants wanted ministries like mine stopped — no matter what. Persuasion didn't work, so their harassment escalated. Their direct action groups attacked our offices three times over an eight month period. They threw paint on the walls. They phoned in death threats almost daily. One morning the Lesbian Avengers dumped jarfuls of locusts onto the carpet, and climbed on our desks, stomping and screaming.

— A refugee

Six days after their reckless flight from Boulder, their faces noticeably thinner and browner than when they began, Vern and John Yates cross the Continental Divide at Arapaho Pass. Vern allows them a satisfied pause at the top, and slips his arm around his son's shoulder, both of them breathing hard in the high, thin air.

Vern looks West, towards his destination, and, at the sight of the massive slopes studding a far turquoise horizon, he feels for the first time in days the warm stirrings of hope.

… demanding a separation between church and state isn't enough; the churches' basic doctrines must be changed, with homophobia written out forever.

Best-selling gay author
Michelangelo Signorile, 1994.

1994. *A Mississippi gay man files suit in federal court against the Oxford University Press demanding both $45 million in damages and the immediate deletion of all Scripture verses describing homosexuality as sinful. "The Bible abused and oppressed me," claims Ford, "when it said homosexuality is a sin, because I was born a homosexual."*

SIX

Two Wednesday nights after the attack on their church, Pastor Miller had called the adult members of the congregation to an emergency service.

Sitting nervously beside Gail, Vern had thought his old friend's face looked pale and worn as he backed away from the pulpit, walked down the steps to floor level, and leaned wearily against the communion table.

"I have a confession to make to you all. As many of you know, when gay rights started becoming such a hot topic, I rejected any organized attempts within our church to oppose it. My motives were pure. I believed that my commitment to sharing the gospel precluded getting involved in political issues. I thought politics and the gospel had nothing to do with each other." He took a long, deep breath and shook his head. "Now, seeing the way our church's ability to share the gospel has been hamstrung by these militant attacks, I realize I was wrong."

Pastor Miller had paused, looking down at the floor. He shook his head and for a moment it appeared he might cry. Then he looked up, his eyes indeed filled with tears. "We've lost the battle, folks."

All of his familiar preaching mannerisms, the strong voice, the sharp gestures, the dramatic hesitations, had left him. He had looked up with a weak smile. "I mean, as Christians, we've definitely won the ultimate war, and we still have the hope of Heaven, but right now ... I confess that for me those hopes are hard to hold on to."

He had wiped his eyes and looked out over the congregation. "Many of you know that several years ago, while I was still in seminary, I made a visit to the Soviet Union. While I was there I worshipped at an underground church in a city called Smolensk, where the pastor knew KGB agents were sitting in the congregation, gathering evidence against him. You see, his words were considered harmful and destructive to the Soviet state. By preaching the gospel he was committing an act of treason against his government — or so they said. They did finally send him to prison, less than three months after I returned. He died five years later at a camp in Siberia. And I remember telling myself, 'Thank God I live in America.'"

He had stopped, as if pondering whether to go on. Then a defiant look had crossed his face and he had continued. "The reason I'm telling you this is that right this second, there are agents among us tonight from the Human Relations Commission, here to monitor my words for hate speech." His mouth had twisted, and anger had flooded his voice. "It is my duty to welcome you in the name of Christ, but actually I just want to ask you — is the Sermon on the Mount hate speech? John 3:16? Does 1 Corinthians 13, the love chapter, does it meet with your approval? Or should I just submit my sermon plan to you in advance so you can make sure I'm politically correct?"

He had paused for a long, deep breath, seemingly embarassed by the digression. He had blown out, a long, tense exhale. "As you know, we've been searching for a youth pastor for quite a long time. Recently, a young man answered our ad. He was clean-cut, had good credentials. He even offered to work for free — which as you know, given our financial shortfall, was an incredibly attractive offer." He stopped, a puzzled, baffled look frozen momentarily upon his face.

"Then he told me he was gay." An audible gasp rippled through the congregation.

"I know you all thought, as I did, that our city's gay rights ordinance had a so-called 'religious exemption.' Well, turns out that exemption has one enormous loophole. Dan, would you explain?"

Dan Oliver, a respected local attorney and long-time church member, had stood from the congregation with a yellow legal pad in his hand. "When you read the fine print, it turns out that the religious exemption in our Boulder ordinance, like most of them out there, only exempts churches and religious groups, 'for the purposes of favoring a member of their denomination.' What that means is that a Baptist church can legally hire a white Baptist applicant over a black Methodist applicant. That's it. I know we thought 'religious exemption' meant that all churches were excluded, period, from the ordinance. It wasn't true."

Pastor Miller cut in. "And as it happens, this gay applicant was educated at a Baptist university, and says he's a Baptist in good standing."

"It appears to have been a setup," Oliver continued. "A deliberate trap to prove a point and destroy this church. He clearly never intended to work for us. And he has filed a complaint against us at the City Commission. Discrimination on the basis of sexual orientation."

This time no sound escaped from the congregation. They sat, frozen in several hundred individual postures of dread and resignation. "So we're left with two choices," Pastor Miller said. "We can spend most of the few funds we have left on legal fees to fight this."

"And face a high probability of losing," Oliver interjected.

"Or, we can vote tonight to dissolve this church into a network of home groups. We would continue as a body of believers, only unofficially. It would break my heart, but..." He had trailed off, looking away, trying to hide his eyes.

That night, at 7:35 on a Wednesday evening, Boulder's Second Baptist Church had ceased to exist.

1993. *After signing the U.N. Covenant on the Rights of the Child, the French government raids seven Christian homes, separating children from their parents, searching property, confiscating documents, arresting adults. Children are interrogated for up to ten hours and permanently placed in a state reeducation center. Because they homeschool, teach religion and occasionally spank, two mothers are imprisoned for five weeks. Parents are denied contact with their children. Parents are told their children wish no communication with them.*

1995. *A Washington journalist sponsors an initiative which would prevent Washington state agencies from placing children in the custody of anyone "who practices right-wing fundamentalist Christianity."*

SEVEN

"**M**ommy, tell me a story."

"Which one, precious?"

"You know. An olden days story."

"Heather, I'm not sure I can right now."

"Please? About the days when we used to go church picnics and play with our friends? And nobody was trying to put Daddy and Johnny in jail?"

"Baby, there's something a lot more important we need to talk about."

"Please?"

"Heather, listen to me. Heather, when the doorbell rings, there's gonna be some people, and they're gonna take you away with them on a trip for a while."

"Are they police? Are they police, Mommy?"

"No, not exactly."

"Mommy ... "

"It's okay. They'll be nice to you. And if the judge is happy with us tomorrow, you can come right home again."

"But what if the judge isn't happy? What about then?"

The woman walks sharply onto the small open space of carpet, looks down, then up again to the judge. Her hands fold before her, as if in prayer.

"For nearly every day of her young life," she says slowly, fixing him with a lowered stare, "Heather Yates has been immersed in one of the most destructive and malicious types of psychological dysfunction in America today." Her head snaps still. "Homophobia."

She speaks the word carefully, all five syllables.

For a second or two, she says nothing else. Then she turns to face Gail Yates at the front table. "It's time for the abuse to stop." She whirls back around, the stare broken. "Your Honor, it's probably too late to rehabilitate her mother here or her fugitive, criminal father. Heather's parents are perfect examples of the kind of unquenchable hate that brought the stain of Amendment 2 onto our state constitution just a few years ago. Coloradans may have put that awful chapter behind us ... but not this family."

Now she walks right up to Gail and leans toward the table. "This family insists on holding on to their outdated, hateful attitudes despite the fact that society has finally left them behind. They cling to their mental illness as if it were a cloak of honor. And your Honor, four-year-old Heather has paid the price."

From beside Gail, another attorney stands at the table. "I suppose it would be futile to point out that these statements are argumentative, purely conjectural, nothing more than vicious invective aimed at my client's beliefs?"

The face behind the flat smoked-glass bench comes to life and turns his way. "Are you objecting, counselor?"

"Trying to, your Honor."

"Overruled."

In the corner of her eye, Gail tracks the form of her attorney sitting down wearily as he has a dozen times today, his deliberate sigh puncturing the air between them. She turns to follow the continued gutting of her family. This woman in silk whose well-paid, white-collar government mission is to strip her daughter away.

All through the day, as the procedural babble has unwound over the hours, as her attorney has led her numbly through the bureaucratic torrent, she has tried to focus on a single terrifying thought — that all this is truly happening. She cannot force her mind into accepting that something as absurd, as senseless as this day, has actually come to pass.

She tries to imagine some anxious friend telling her, ten years ago, when she could still recognize the country she'd grown up in, that today she would be sitting in a court of law facing the probability of losing her beloved daughter. And not for some sort of abuse or molestation, but for the crime of teaching her traditional beliefs. She would have laughed in the friend's face. "Oh, get a life," she would have told her. "These kinds of things don't happen in America. You're getting a little paranoid, you know? You've been reading too much conservative direct mail ..."

The Department of Social Services lawyer speaks again.

"Your honor, as you well know, this has been going on for a long time now. The Yates family has already been ordered, by this very court, to bring their children's home schooling into compliance with state multicultural curriculum guidelines."

The judge nods. The attorney motions to the sidelines, "Bailiff, the monitor ..." She turns back to the bench as a large television stand is rolled out into the room. "Yet, as this video will show, Gail Yates continues to defy both the court's instruction and the state's guidelines for teaching her children."

The glowing screen reveals a beautiful child's face, blond hair with large blue eyes. A voice comes from behind the camera, adult, soothing.

"Heather, what does your mommy teach you about families?"

"She ..." The blues eyes wander. "Mommy says God gave families for having babies and taking care of 'em and lovin 'em."

"Tell me about those families Mommy talks about."

"Well, there's a mommy, and a daddy, and then babies, children, like Johnny and me."

"Okay, Heather. Now I'm gonna give you some dolls to play with."

A hand extends from outside the frame, holding six dolls. Four of them large, adults. Two small child dolls. Heather's gaze falls as she takes them and begins playing.

"You have a family there, don't you?" the adult voice asks.

"Uh-huh."

"Tell me about your family."

"Well, here's Mommy, here's Daddy, and here's me and Johnny." She pulls two male dolls out of the group. "This is Daddy and Johnny. They're gone away right now. Cause it's not safe for them to be at home." Heather looks intently off-camera at her questioner. "But Daddy's coming back to get us, to take us where it's safe."

"Oh." The adult voice pauses. "Now today, Heather, we have other kinds of families. Did you know that?"

"Well, sure. There's the Johansens, and the Taylors on the corner, and the McGraws ..."

"No, that's not what I mean. I'm talking about completely *different* kinds of families."

Heather says nothing. Soon two adult hands enter the frame again and shuffle the dolls. Heather is left with two men and a child in one hand, two female adult dolls in the other.

"What do you think, Heather? Do you think this is a family? A family you'd like to be a part of?"

Heather giggles. Obviously, this adult is making a joke. "You're being silly. God didn't make families like that. Families are supposed to be a mommy and a daddy."

The screen goes gray and loud. The lawyer steps in

front of it, the merest hint of a smile playing upon her face.

"Your honor, the learned prejudices you've just seen, although coming from the innocent heart of a girl, actually mark the early stages of heterosexism. Of homophobia. Everything our state's multicultural curriculum was designed to eliminate. This is a family totally out of compliance."

Gail turns away. She feels her shoulders, her hands and feet shaking. She cannot stop them. She knows enough of the law to realize the case against her has just been sealed. Inside, she starts to bid her daughter good-bye.

"Mommy, the doorbell."

"I know, baby."

"Are you gonna get it? Huh? Is it ... is it those people come to get me, Mommy?"

Gail feels herself walking to the door, watches her hand reach out and turn the knob, open it. A blinding, nauseating rush engulfs her head as she recognizes the social worker, grim and still in flowered skirt and sandals. The familiar watch policeman stands behind her.

"Now baby, you be nice to these people. They're gonna take you on a little vacation. Remember, your Dad and I love you. We're gonna come get you."

"They're not taking me on vacation. They're gonna take me to jail."

The social worker bends down into Heather's face with a broad, warm smile. "Little girls don't go to jail, honey. We're gonna go to a nice school where you'll play with lots of nice boys and girls ..."

"If the judge says, honey," Gail interrupts. "Only if the judge says. Otherwise, you'll be back home in a few days."

The other woman's eyes dart upward to Gail's. "Oh yeah."

She hands Heather the little white suitcase, bought for last year's family vacation and now packed with as many clothes as she could fit inside. Then through a blur she watches her little girl, in her best Sunday dress, walking down the pathway toward the street. The social worker offers to carry the suitcase but Heather shakes her head, "No." The woman tries to take her hand; Heather lets her for a second and then drops it. The little girl turns around. Gail tries to wipe her face clear for a last look.

"Bye, Mommy …"

Gail breaks from the memory back to the sound of the lawyer's voice.

"Heather was not given the choice of which family to be born into, your Honor. The law is quite clear on the issue of subjecting children to these kinds of archaic values. Hatred and bigotry. This family has been given ample opportunity to correct its behavior. And has steadfastly refused. The law offers no excuses for denying any child the multicultural curriculum. Home schooled or otherwise. The State is obligated to free little Heather from this prison, your Honor."

The judge nods. "Miss Yates, please approach the bench. With your attorney." His voice now rings with finality. Gail finds herself standing, staring upward at his face.

"Ma'am, your daughter is going to become a temporary ward of the state. Do you understand that? Young lady? Are you all right?"

Gail finds that her head is shaking side to side, telling him, *No. No! I'm not okay, and it's not okay, what's going on here.*

"Temporary ward of the state means we're going to continue holding Heather in custody, and we're going to care for her while we evaluate whether you and your husband are capable of ever properly parenting your children."

"Your Honor," the prosecutor interrupts. "The husband is a fugitive from the law right now. With kidnapping aggravating the charge, to boot."

"Wait a minute," Gail's lawyer snaps. "He's fled with his son. That's not kidnapping."

"It is when the child's treatment is under investigation."

Her lawyer shakes his head. The judge holds up his hand. "This isn't the issue right now, folks. I'm awarding Miss Yates here bimonthly visits with Heather at the New School. Under supervision of a worker, of course. But Ma'am, I have to warn you." Gail doesn't even look up. "If you so much as utter a peep about your homophobic beliefs during your visits with Heather, I'll terminate your visitation rights just like that. Maybe for good. Do you understand?" He waits. "Do you understand me, Ma'am?"

She doesn't answer. Before the rage explodes from her, she turns and walks away. Halfway across the courtroom floor she starts to run, slowly. She passes the bailiff staring at the judge for instructions, and leaves him behind.

Outside the sky is blue, the grass green, just as it always was. Just the way things used to be. Gail Yates keeps running, running towards home, and through the anger she begins to understand why her husband left, never looked behind, and simply ran for the hills.

1992. *The* Denver Post *reports Denver public school teachers face pressure to teach that homosexuality is normal, beginning in kindergarten.*

66

Is it possible your heterosexuality is just a phase you may outgrow? How can you hope to become a whole person if you ... remain unwilling to explore and develop your normal, natural, healthy, homosexual potential?

99

Question # 14 for public school students contained in a teacher's guide entitled "Gay and Lesbian Youth Tools for Educators," given to Denver area teachers in 1992.

EIGHT

One cool Thursday morning in Fraser, Colorado, a town separated from Boulder by eighty miles, two mountain ranges and the Continental Divide, Pastor Greg Johnson opens the door of the sanctuary and spots two dark, reclining shapes on the carpet, near the back of the room.

Homeless people are not unheard of, even in this small mountain town. He turns away and returns ten minutes later, bearing coffee cups and a cardboard box of stale donuts.

He soon learns his two intruders are not vagrants.

Within the hour the three are driving south in the pastor's weathered Ford pickup.

It occurs to Vern, as he keeps his eyes fixed through the windshield for police lights atop passing cars, that the man seems to have made this drive before.

Vern thinks back to the moment he became an activist.

The previous July. A microphone switches on with a whine, then a woman's solemn, official voice rings out across a packed auditorium.

"As you all know, we're here tonight for this open forum to discuss the proposed curriculum changes for Boulder's public schools. I want to caution the audience tonight, since there are so many of you —" she pauses and looks sternly through the top of her bifocals at the assembled crowd before her, "that we are here for rational discussion, and insults, unseemly outbursts, or attempts to silence opponents, will not be tolerated. We will behave as civilized people."

Four rows back sit Vern and Gail and their two young children, dressed up for the evening, attentive and watchful, and most of all — terrified. All around them seethes a roiling mass of assembled hostility, an ocean of resentment surging from a thousand eyes, plastered across mouths and faces. Vern imagines all that fury directed at him five minutes from now, when he stands there to give his statement. Scanning the crowd, Vern sees perhaps a dozen parents he knows opposed to the Children of the Rainbow curriculum. That's all.

A young woman in her early twenties speaks, her voice wracked with stage fright and overwrought indignation. "Ladies and gentlemen of the board, I cannot tell you how much I needed the affirmation of this kind of program, when I was a lesbian high school student. I can't imagine how much pain and heartache and how many lost years of my life I could have avoided if only I could have been told, 'Yes, Danielle, you are different and it *is* okay ...' Please don't give in to the forces of hate and intolerance. Give the youth of our city a chance to discover themselves. Please."

Bathed in applause, she backs away from the microphone. Even Vern can see the attractiveness of his opponents' rhetoric. *Everybody wants to feel they're on the side of tolerance and openness and pluralism ... even if they're not on that side at all ...*

Then he sees a gray-haired man in his early seventies, gray slacks and an ill-fitting navy blazer. He fiddles interminably with a thick sheath of papers. "Ladies and gentlemen," he says after a racking cough, in a low, tobacco-roughened voice, "I beseech you not to give in to the abomination of homosexuality, which the Lord clearly condemns in the Bible ..."

Vern winces and looks down, darkly meeting Gail's gaze. *Why do we always seem to dig up our worst communicators for times like these?* Already competing with a rising chorus of jeers, the man continues. "This is the reason God ordained that a family consist of a man and a woman..."

The clamor rises further and a gavel rings sharply across the room. "People, I warned you that this sort of behavior will not be tolerated. And sir, we are here to consider public policy concerns related to the introduction of sexual orientation into school curricula. I would ask you to confine your remarks to matters of pertinence to our board. This is not, after all, a church meeting ..."

The man stares at her, his script still held high in a weathered hand. Whether he is enraged or merely considering his options, no one can tell. Suddenly he turns around and walks down the aisle to a chorus of catcalls, the activists seemingly incited by his wordless surrender.

"Now, our next statement ..."

The immaculately coiffed young woman carries no paper. She confines the motions of her hand to smooth strokes along the narrow sides of her designer suit, smoothing the tight-fitting grey flannel around her hips. "As the Colorado representative for the National Education Association, which is of course the nation's lobby for children's education ..." — she looks around the room, as if to verify that her importance has sufficiently registered — "I want to express the complete confidence of our nation's educational experts in the quality and appropriateness of the Rainbow Curriculum. I frankly find it outrageous that parents who know nothing of this program's substance would try to stop it merely because it mentions homosexuality and sexual behavior."

Vern is out of his seat, marching up to the microphone behind her with his prepared statement in hand. "It is a shocking reminder that ignorance and bigotry remain with us, even after all the bitter lessons of history. And yet it's proof once more of how vitally important education remains to our survival. We must educate hatred and homophobia out of existence. Thank you."

She almost bumps into Vern in her haste to leave the stand. Once again the room is engulfed by loud waves of applause. He waits a minute for the auditorium to grow quiet.

"Next, Mr. Vernon ..."

"Yates. I just want to say that I am a Christian who believes gays and lesbians should have every equal right accorded to American citizens." A smattering of applause from the other side — *a Christian who supports us!* "I personally know and appreciate many gay friends at work and in the community. However, as someone who also personally believes homosexuality to be wrong, I cannot abide ..." Angry shrieks of betrayal drown him out, then the fierce pounding of the gavel — "... cannot abide having my tax dollars used to indoctrinate my children into a belief system that not only flies directly against my most cherished values, but also concerns a subject area that's none of the school district's business. How can you justify, when our math and science scores and our literacy rates are at an all-time low, spending time and money to teach kids how to sodomize each other?"

A man in his early twenties, thin, clad in bicycle shorts and a lavender t-shirt, stands and shouts. "You evil bigot, our lives *are* the school district's business!"

The gavel pounds once more. "Sir, one more outburst

But the protester's head bobs up again. "I will not be silenced!" he shouts. "Silence equals death!" And this time it's not applause but a riot of approbation — the crowd leaps to its feet with a deafening roar that soon surges into an angry chant.

"*Silence equals death! Silence equals death! Silence equals death!*"

Vern turns to the school board panel but they too are undone by the display of rage. They shake their heads, cover their ears. The pounding gavel cannot be heard.

"Why can't we calmly disagree?" Vern asks into the microphone, his voice inaudible. He feels like continuing, like staying right there and speaking the truth until this mob has spent its rage. "Why is it you can't allow me to have a difference of opinion without painting me as a hate monger or a bigot?" He looks back to Gail but she remains rooted in her seat, her eyes locked on him. "This is America! What happened to civil discourse?"

The chanting only grows louder. Outnumbered, the lone deputy holds his radio up to his mouth and appears to speak. Vern feels a hand grip his, tightly. At last Gail leads him away, towards the calm of the night air.

The next day Vern sees his picture in the paper, sees himself neatly summarized in print. "Religious right activist." The following month, when the Rainbow Curriculum becomes required study in public schools, Gail's home-schooling endeavors hit the ground running.

And for the first time, Vern begins to feel that his culture has leaped over the precipice.

*Some people may need professional help to
deal with their phobia of gay or lesbian people,
just as some need help to deal with fear of heights
or elevators.*

Pamphlet entitled, *Homophobia: What Are We So
Afraid Of?* distributed in schools by the Lesbian and
Gay Public Awareness Project, compliments
of National Coming Out Day, 1993.

NINE

CHILD WELFARE INTAKE REPORT
HEATHER YATES
Age 4, D.O.B. 2/14/96
Boulder County, Boulder, CO

PRESENTING PROBLEM: Child being home schooled in a right-wing, homophobic home. Retarded awareness-development due to continuous exposure to extremist beliefs. Educational neglect resulting from parental failure to adhere to Multicultural Curriculum guidelines. Social worker rates overall home environment at Unacceptable, Severity Level 7.

PARENTAL CUSTODY REINSTATEMENT PLAN: Mother, Gail, age 36, ordered by Family Court on March 23, 1998 to undergo sensitivity training as part of Custody Reinstatement plan. First session with the Sensitivity Services Inc., of Boulder scheduled within two weeks. Failure to follow the Plan of a complete, 6-session Sensitivity Course will result in immediate termination of parental rights without hearing.

CURRENT STATUS: Minor child remanded to custody of New School for foster care and reeducation until outcome of Parental Custody Reinstatement.

Through the van's rear window, Heather watches the ridge of mountains behind Boulder grow smaller and less distinct. The big rocks she has known all her life, the ones her Mommy calls "Flatirons," have disappeared. The countryside now lies flat, fields stretching all the way to the sky.

Now, just before the mountaintops vanish behind the horizon, the van stops before a very large gate. Behind it stand three sprawling buildings that look like houses, only much bigger, much longer. Before them spreads the biggest yard she's ever seen, with playgrounds and swing sets and children.

The fear of this brand new place overwhelms her — such big buildings and strange children and unknown grown-ups. She wants to be a big girl, but now she cannot help the tears or the sobbing noises her mouth is making. If only Mommy was here. Then everything would be all right.

Theresa Knowles kneels in front of the little girl's chair. Intake interviews are the only time she bothers to do this when talking to the children. Too hard on her knees. The little girl is distracted. Beyond the window, a dozen children sit on the New School's bright green lawn, singing the tune of "Jesus Loves the Little Children," but with strange words Heather has never heard before.

"Heather, you've gotten some new toys today, haven't you?"

"Uh-huh. I got a new stuffed pony and a doll and a coloring set."

"And you got some new friends too, didn't you?"

"Yeah. I met Rhonda and Suzi and Laurel. They're gonna be in my room."

"Rhonda and Suzi and Laurel sound like new sisters, don't they?"

"Uh-huh. I've never had a sister."

"You're gonna love it. Nina here is gonna be taking care of you. She's gonna be like a ... well, like a new Mommy to you."

Theresa lays a hand on the girl's arm, gathering in her attention.

"A new house to live in, a new Mommy, new brothers and sisters. What does that sound like you got? What does all that sound like, Heather? Mommy, brother, sister ..."

"A new family."

"That's exactly right. You're getting a new family." Theresa now takes both the girl's hands in hers. "See, it's like with toys. Sometimes little-girl toys wear out and become too old to play with. That's because they're not safe anymore. When that happens, it's time to get big-girl toys. Nice, big, new ones. Even though we loved the old ones a whole lot."

Theresa moves in even closer. "Heather, your old family wasn't safe for you anymore. Since it's our job to make sure you're safe, we decided it was time to give you a new one. A new family where you can play whenever you want to, and make lots of new friends, and learn a lot of new, wonderful things. Does that sound fun, Heather?"

The large blue eyes flutter slightly, uncertain. "Yeah."

While I read the verse I started hearing hissing. It got louder and louder, and pretty soon out of the corner of my eye I saw that two of them were standing and had put whistles to their mouths. By the time I'd finished my verse, condoms were flying across the sanctuary.

— A refugee

Blinking in the bright spring sunshine that streams through the classroom windows, Heather stands before the room, clasps her hands before her and sings the Diversity Song for the first time, in a thin plaintive voice.

We love all the little children
All the children of the world
Red and yellow, straight and gay
We are not afraid to play
When we love the little children of the world ...

The teacher applauds, along with all the children. Heather feels so happy. If only Mommy — her *old* Mommy — were there to see her.

Today she's playing dolls with her new friends, sprawled out on the carpeted floor. Nina's heavy footsteps pause behind her. She hears her clothes rustle as the woman crouches, the big voice in her ear. "Okay. I think it's time to play with a new kind of family. That's a good family you made there, Heather, but can anyone make us a different one?"

Laurel reaches in. She throws the woman doll into the corner with an impulsive toss. Reaching behind her into a pile, she pulls out another man doll and places it beside the first. "Here."

"That's right, Laurel. Very good." She has made excellent progress. She's healed from her homophobic parents' values more rapidly than any student in a year or more. "Heather, what kind of a family is that?"

"A gay family."

"That's right. And that's a good family too, isn't it?"

The children erupt in a giggly chorus of yesses and affirmations. They're getting it. "Okay. It sure is." Nina stands and pulls her next teaching tool from a shirt pocket. Holding it up, she asks, "This family has two daddies. And does anyone remember what these two daddies use when they love each other?"

Suzi raises her hand and says the word awkwardly. "A condom."

Leaning far back in her office chair, Theresa hardly looks up at Gail Yates from the legal document. "Mrs. Yates, I see here you missed your second meeting of Sensitivity Training."

Gail pauses for a second. Her memory of that first night flashes before her. A yellow-lit classroom. Two fellow students, the three of them addressed like children by a series of angry, masculine women. Then the lights dimming. A scene of two naked women writhing on the video screen. Low voices telling her, Watch it. Don't look down. Don't look down, you homophobe. She chases the memory away.

"Yes." Gail tells the bureaucrat. "I did not return."

"You realize that the Reinstatement Plan is the only way for you to regain custody of Heather."

Gail fixes her with a stare. "How could I not realize that, Ms. Knowles."

"Well, our staff's worked very hard to give Heather a proper diversity awareness. And I'll tell you right now, we're not gonna undo all her progress by just handing her back into a psychologically abusive home. Do you understand that?"

"Yes I do. Can I see my child now ..."

"Sure. It doesn't matter anyway. One more missed meeting, and it says here your rights will be terminated automatically. So ... come with me."

Finally the door opens and there stands her daughter, only twenty feet away. All the time and pain disappears in a blur of Heather running toward her, the word "Mommy" cried out in that once-so-familiar voice, the small form leaping into her arms. She hugs her beloved daughter as tightly as she dares.

She stands and it's not a dream, Heather's still there clutching her. It amazes her that after all that's happened all the tiniest things remain the same: the touching way the little-girl hands grasp a loop of her hair, how the small feet curl up around her waist when she holds her. Their mutual instincts have returned in an instant.

"How are you, baby?" she speaks into the mass of blond hair against her chest.

Heather only hugs her again, tighter. As Theresa Knowles turns and leaves with a grim smile, Nina motions them outside.

She strides across the perfect grass, still holding her daughter. "See over there, Mommy? That's where my room is."

"Oh. Do you like it?"

"Yeah, but Suzi snores at night. She's loud. She's my friend."

"Have you made lots of new friends?"

"Uh-huh." The blue eyes look into hers. "Mommy ...?"

"Yes, Heather?"

"Have Daddy and Johnny come back to get us yet?"

Gail looks down at the ground. She senses Nina silent behind them, watching her closely for the answer.

"No honey. Daddy and Johnny are still missing up in the mountains."

"Are they gonna come back for us?"

"Heather, I don't know."

Nina comes to life. "Heather, why don't you tell Mommy some of the things you've learned."

"Oh yeah. I've learned about rainbow families, and accepting people, and oh yeah, I've learned the Diversity Song." Heather suddenly frowns. "You were wrong, Mommy."

"Wrong about what, sweetheart?"

"About how God makes families. God makes 'em sometimes with two daddies or two mommies, too."

Gail feels her breathing constrict. She looks over at Nina. The other woman's face is set on professional mode, watching her intently. No trace of sympathy.

"Next year, I get to take a test to see if I'm gay or straight. Which do you think I am, Mommy? Huh? Which do you think?"

Gail's mind goes blank. She cannot let the rage escape. She stares at the ground and holds her girl tighter. Finally Nina intervenes. "Heather, would you like some lunch?

Does that sound good?"

"Yeah!" Heather squirms out of Gail's arms and runs across the grass toward a nearby picnic table.

Following her, Gail turns to Nina. "This is wrong," she says in a low voice. "You have no right to take my child and fill her with propaganda that's against everything we believe in."

Nina answers without looking at her. "What you believe doesn't matter anymore. Your beliefs are bigoted, and bigotry isn't tolerated in today's America."

Gail doesn't reply. She has no reply to give. They reach the table and sit down beside Heather, who has already begun tearing into three brown lunch bags waiting there. The little girl holds up a sandwich and prepares to bite down. Gail touches her shoulder.

"Heather, what do we do before eating?"

She stops, looks at her mother. Her eyes are blank. "Who do we thank before our meals?" The eyes narrow again; the memory returns. Heather bows her head and begins to speak. "Thank you Jesus ..."

But a hand grasps her arm and Nina interrupts in a flat voice, "Honey, you don't have to do that. No one can make you do that here."

Heather looks at her. "But ..."

"I'm not making her ..."

"You're withholding the girl's food unless she performs this fundamentalist ritual."

"Oh my God! What is going on?"

Nina turns swiftly into Heather's face. "Why don't you go play with your friends now, Heather?"

"But I don't want to ..."

"Go." The order rings flat upon the little girl's features. Nina pulls her from the bench and sets her down facing back towards the building. "Karen," she calls across the lawn, "would you come over and take Heather for me? Over to the playground?"

Another social worker comes over, sweeps Heather into

her arms, and walks away. Gail hears her little girl's wail across the distance. Nina turns to her, her face tight. "Mrs. Yates, I thought we were clear about the consequences of any fundamentalist indoctrination on your part."

"A prayer before lunch is fundamentalist indoctrination?" Gail's voice now grows to a shout. "Come on!"

"Yes. It is. This visit is concluded, ma'am. I'll have to ask you to leave the premises."

Numb, Gail stands. There's no use.

Not until she's driven beyond the gate does she break. She pulls beside the road two hundred feet beyond and slumps over in the seat, too wracked even for tears.

An hour later a security guard investigates the seemingly abandoned vehicle and finds her still lying prone across the seat, weeping.

"Heather, I have something to tell you."

"What?"

"Your Mommy hasn't gone to Training like the judge asked her to."

"Oh."

"Now there's no way your old family's gonna be safe for you to go back to. It's okay, Heather. You don't have to cry."

Nina gathers her in for a hug. "Old Mommy's lost her parental rights, Heather. And that means you're gonna stay with us for a while. Then later we're gonna find you a new home for good. For your whole life. A home that's safe."

"So, Old Mommy doesn't love me anymore?"

66

... businesses will fail, people will be fired for feelings or beliefs about homosexuality, because homosexuals will claim persecution and discrimination. Your freedom of speech will be violated. These are all costly enough as it is. But your children, your grandchildren, they will be taught the 'virtues of homosexual lifestyles.' They will be counseled further into mental illness and untold thousands will die ...

99

"A Warning to Heterosexuals"
from Jeff (a pseudonym), a former homosexual,
writing from New Mexico, 1993.

TEN

One beautiful spring afternoon, on a trail high in the Sawatch range of the Rocky Mountains, two figures round a sharp curve and stop at the sudden panorama of an alpine valley spreading to the sheer wall of the Continental Divide. Vern stops and grasps his son by the shoulder. There under an ice-blue sky, three snow-dusted peaks tower above plunging forests and a deep, thickly wooded gorge.

He speaks, still huffing softly. "The Three Apostles."

"Is that them, Daddy?"

He points. "Up there. Those three mountain tops. You see 'em?"

The boy squints and nods. The peaks' jagged magnificence makes him feel so tiny.

"This is where we're going?"

"Uh-huh."

At the sight of this place, Vern finally feels the enormity of his gamble. He has brought Johnny here because of two hushed sentences whispered hurriedly into his ear nearly six months ago. Another father soon to disappear into the wilds with his family had relented after fifteen minutes of Vern's pressured questioning. The man had leaned his thin form over a diner's formica tabletop and whispered once, "The Apostles, Vern. Find the Apostles and you'll find the Refuge." He had stood up then, shaken his hand and walked off. Vern had never seen him again.

The Apostles. At first Vernon had taken it for a scriptural or theological reference. He had stayed up six nights in a row, scanning his Bible's use of "apostles." He had printed them all neatly on yellow note cards and taped them above his tiny desk in a corner of the bedroom. He had prayed for insight. He had meditated on a reference every single day. None pointed him toward any real, specific place where he and his family would find Refuge.

Finally he'd gone to his pastor to ask if he had perhaps overlooked some obscure Greek or Aramaic reference. Pastor Miller's eyes had fallen, the pitch of his voice had lowered, and Vern immediately realized that his pastor's knowledge of the subject ran far deeper than he'd imagined. "You're making it too hard, Vern," the pastor had muttered lamely. "It's far more simple than that. It's geography — not theology."

Two days later, in a fit of stubborn desperation, he felt his eyes freeze over a tiny spot of a Colorado map.

The Three Apostles.

The small italicized print curved slightly over a section of the wandering Continental Divide, southwest of Leadville. A large, knowing smile had spread over his face and his insides, as if he'd already known somehow for hours or days. The object of his search had been three adjacent peaks overlooking a long valley studded with lakes, old mines and ghost towns. He had climbed into bed smiling that night — at last, the knowledge that would help his family reach safety. Knowledge that could send him to jail.

Today standing here, that old confidence feels foolish and premature, as a cold wind tugs at him and he realizes he has no idea what to do in this valley. Climb the Apostles? They look rugged and steep; a challenge even for technical climbers. No way would he even consider it with a young boy alongside. And how could Refuge be located there, anyhow? They are in a Wilderness Area, a federally designated stretch of land with no roads, no buildings, no motor vehicles allowed. Should he wander around the valley bottom, yelling for help? Not a chance. Anybody in the area could hear him, including government patrols. *Come on God. Let me know what to do here.* No answer. He knows of no other option but to continue. One foot in front of another, praying help will reach them before they die of exposure.

They set off again down the worn mountain trail, skirting a stream shrouded in occasional snow patches and the flat surfaces of beaver ponds. With a shift of the breeze, sunshine floods the valley and they begin to hear, once more, the pleasant gurgle of water.

From his high mountain perch, the two tiny forms seem to crawl in trembling binocular sights.

Man, mid-thirties. Young boy, maybe ten.

The boy watching knows this is an illusion of distance, that figures in motion always appear to move slower when observed from great heights. But he has also watched dozens of hikers on this trail over the past eight months. He can judge. These two are weary; bone-tired. They've walked far longer than just two miles from the Wilderness trailhead. He lowers the binoculars to a chunk of rock at his feet and raises a small black wand to his mouth. He speaks a few words in a near whisper. Twenty yards away, another boy's head appears suddenly. The first watcher points downward. Another set of lenses begins scanning the worn ribbon of trail two thousand feet below.

Thirty minutes later Vern's heart rate leaps to a runaway gallop, a split second before his brain registers the presence of another hiker behind them on the trail. Touching Johnny on the shoulder, he bends over with his heavy pack and grasps his knees, feigning an exhausted break. His peripheral vision confirms the existence of their visitor. He's alone: a boy about thirteen, carrying a light brown backpack. Vern turns towards their follower and the boy stops, eyes darting across their faces, their equipment, their clothes. Vern senses something he likes from this boy: a strong, level gaze, freckles across a tanned face, a purposeful stance. Finally, the newcomer smiles.

"Hi, you guys."

Johnny manages a small "Hi." His face is still scrunched together; he's having a harder time evaluating the hiker's character than his father.

"Where you headed?"

Vern jerks his chin outwards, towards the valley. "Oh, you know ..."

The hiker seems almost surprised. His eyes follow Vern's to the Apostles. "You headed to Lake Marie?"

"Yeah. That's where we're going. Camp, do some fishing."

The boy leans back at those words, his gaze leaving them abruptly.

Vern can see the boy is doing some fast thinking. Then in a red-hot flash the thought bursts upon him: *there is no Lake Marie. There's a Lake Ann ... the boy's testing me.*

Their eyes meet and hold. A very long pause passes between them. Long enough for Vern to sense for certain that the boy is on their side, there to help them — and desperately trying to decide whether they're trustworthy. The stakes must be so enormous ...

"You're a Scout, aren't you, Son." Vern uses his deepest father's voice.

The boy locks onto him. "Sir, the Young Scouts of

America teams have been officially disbanded in pursuance of Court Order ... "

"I know that." Vern interrupts. "We all know that." He almost smiles, for the little speech and the cold fire in the boy's eyes confirm exactly what his heart's been telling him. No remaining, active Scout can admit to official membership since that fateful day a year-and-a-half ago when a Massachusetts federal judge ordered them to admit as Scoutmaster a member of the pedophile "Man-Boy Love" organization. The national leadership had defied the order and within hours found themselves facing contempt charges. Twenty minutes later a restraining order had shut down every troop in the nation. Scouting had become a crime in the timespan of an afternoon nap. "Not even a cherished institution may be allowed to discriminate on the basis of sexual orientation ... ," thirty-one-year-old Judge LaRonda Washington had droned judicially at the TV cameras in her slow, affected African accent. Most of America had learned an entirely new and frightening fact that day: that "sexual orientation" not only referred to homosexuality, but to any sexual behavior with whom someone chose to identify. The Queer Alliance contingent in the courtroom had erupted into a prolonged celebration dance, requiring extra bailiffs to dispel. And that night, Vern had watched network commentators announce the ascension of brave, young Judge Washington, a mere nine years out of politically correct Sarah Lawrence College, to the president's short list of potential Supreme Court nominees.

Years of tradition, illegalized with the stroke of a pen.

Only most of the Scouts hadn't disbanded at all. Almost immediately, as if by plan, teams had gone underground. They had found a purpose even their enemies could never have imagined: helpers of the newly oppressed, the essential glue for a resistance network spreading like wildfire across the country. If you encountered a Scout these days and were bold enough to ask, he would answer with a faint smile and a litany written in secret by lawyers. "The Young Scouts of America are officially disbanded ... "

And that's how you knew.

"No, son," Vern says. "I'm asking about you. Are you a Scout? Cause me and my boy could sure use some help."

The Scout frowns, his eyes turned away from theirs. Vernon steps forward and offers his hand. "Vern Yates. From Boulder. And this is my son John."

The boy returns the handshake. "My name's Tom. Is this your whole family?"

"No. The Agents raided our house while my wife and daughter were away. I ... " Feeling the boy's eyes upon him, Vern realizes that his voice is shaking badly. "I didn't have time ... "

The boy's eyes bore a hole through his. He begins nodding his head slowly, up and down. He understands. He believes them. All at once his back is turned and he's off at a quick stride away from the path, his voice trailing behind him. "Come on, follow me. We've been out here too long already."

They fight for a moment through a stand of willows until a faint game trail appears, heading up the slope of a huge, barren mountain flanking the valley's eastern edge. Vern had hardly noticed it in his fascination with the Apostles. "Mount Huron. A fourteener," Tom tells them as they stand, looking up the slope. Like most natives, Vern is familiar with the nickname given to the fifty-two Colorado peaks which tower above fourteen thousand feet. "Listen," Tom continues. "We're going to be exposed out there, so we gotta hurry. It's a thousand feet up. Rough climb." He steps out into the open and waves three times to an invisible target high above them. And without another word, their climb begins.

It's an arduous hike, over rocks that slide and shift with every step. The alpine landscape begins to spread behind him, while his breathing grows heavy and labored. Soon he feels a touch upon his palm and it's Johnny, taking his hand the way he once had years ago, as a toddler. They climb through the long minutes, silent except for their breathing and the fierce alpine wind gusts.

Finally he gains his second wind, along with the presence of mind to steal a glance about him now and then. It occurs to him that they're in the sky. A small plane reaching this altitude would be turning on the oxygen. Everywhere around he sees peaks — near and far, foreground and horizon, each one studded with endless detail of forests, cliffs, valleys and streams. He could take a day just drinking it all in, and the effort of looking away frustrates him. He catches fleeting glimpses of white shapes on nearby slopes: mountain goats, reclusive citizens of the high peaks.

They are almost at timberline when Tom stops in front of a thick growth of low, gnarled pine trunks, looks around quickly, crouches and disappears into the side of the mountain. Stunned, Vern and Johnny walk forward to the sight of a neat arched hole, carved from the rock. An abandoned mine shaft! Out in the wilderness. A century ago an army of men with gold rush fever had scoured these mountains for every trace of gold and precious minerals. Finding this place was a stroke of genius. Vern tightens his grip on his son's hand and the two step inside.

"Heads up! Newcomers!" Tom's voice echoes down a rocky passageway. He is still walking. A long row of faces looks up, dim in the opening's scarce light. The wind's whine has ceased. All is now damp, cool and dark. Disoriented and panting, the two step over feet and sleeping bags, duck abruptly to avoid overhanging rocks, trying to stay in sight of their leader's receding form. John's hold upon his father's hand tightens like a vice. Vern turns to him and sees his son's eyes wide with fright.

"Come on, son. I'll be right here in front of you."

Tom turns on a flashlight and for a hundred yards or

more they follow the dancing beam, picking their way along the shaft. They catch up at last as Tom begins inching his way through a shoulder width crawl space between the rock wall and a yawning, roped-off darkness just beside their feet.

"Be careful," Tom whispers, shining briefly into a bottomless chasm. "Slip here, and it'll be ninety seconds before you hit bottom." They turn left into another passageway. Tom hands them a rope to hang onto and they walk for what seems forever. Johnny's teeth begin to chatter in the darkness. Another turn left, one right, and Vern almost collides with Tom's back. He's standing still. Vern hears a knock on hollow steel and, muffled by walls of rock, the humming of a generator. A door creaks and then a bright wedge of light rushes out to meet them.

Still blinking, they enter a large room lit from three light bulbs hanging from a rock ceiling. Boxes and crates fill the space; straw lines the floor. A large map of North America covers most of the far wall. Three middle-aged men at a large table turn at the intrusion. Tom raises his hand.

"Hi, I have two newcomers. Vern and ...?"

"John," Vern answers.

"Vern and John."

A tall, athletic man with white hair and red jogging shorts stands and extends a large hand. "Welcome. I'm Bruce. Have a seat."

The two take chairs, still dazed. Vern remembers part of the lore he has overheard — a tall, brilliant ex-Air Force officer who single-handedly designed and built an elaborate fugitive escape system.

A hand sets down paper cups before he and John, pours water from a plastic pitcher. It feels so strange to have someone serving him, after all this time spent running like a dog. For a minute all Vern knows is the coolness flowing down his throat. His long draught ends and Bruce is still before him, smiling.

"You've been on the run a couple weeks now ... "

Vern feels his eyes go blank. Isn't it unbelievable, to forget how long it has been? He thinks back, over the succession of grim nights and huddled days, his numb acquaintance with asphalt, access lanes and roadside trash.

"Two, yeah, two weeks, I guess."

"You're Vern, the fugitive from Boulder."

"Uh-huh."

"Welcome to the Network. Your days of running alone are over."

Their tour begins back in the darkened tunnel, Vern and John stumbling to keep pace with their energetic host. "We're usually more organized than this," Bruce says, walking briskly. "Normally, we know in advance when someone's coming. We arrange it, we have time to plan, and come up with an exit strategy for every family, sometimes before they've even arrived."

Vern gives him a wry smile. "Sorry. Next time Social Services tries to arrest me, I'll have them make an appointment."

"Don't get me wrong; you know we're glad to have you — I just didn't want you to think it always works this way." As they walk further into the gloom, Bruce palms the walls occasionally, as if orienting himself by touch. "I retired from the Air Force a few years back. And like a lot of people, I realized what was about to start happening."

"I didn't," Vern mumbles grimly.

"Well, my intelligence training taught me to look around and read the signs carefully. But it wasn't enough just to know what was ahead — I felt like I had to do something about it. I'm a big Civil War buff, so I started reading up on the Underground Railroad that helped the fugitive slaves get to freedom. And I figured, what with the technology we have today, and a little bit of planning, we oughta be able to set up something spectacular. A modern version. The Underground Bullet Train, if you will."

They turn into a darkened chamber. Bruce bends along a wall and with a click, overhead lights flicker on, humming softly. "For electricity, I found an advanced photovoltaic generator, using solar energy. I rigged up the panels in the ruins of the mine outbuildings on the far side of the mountain, all mixed in with piles of rusted sheet metal so no one could spot them from the air. Then we ran some buried cable through the tunnel system ..."

Bruce points to stacks of cables and electronics equipment lying in neat piles. "I raised money for several years so we could buy the best. Radio headsets, scrambled frequencies. Nightvision goggles for the sentries. Long-range motion detectors. Laser sights. Cellular comlinks with our help on the outside. We have weapons, but for now the emphasis is on detection, evasion and escape. Who knows about the future? Someday, we may have to take up arms and die for the same freedoms our forefathers died for. I'm praying that day doesn't come."

He pauses a moment, looking away into the shadows, then flicks off the lights and leads them to a back passage they haven't walked before. "We kept two rooms all prepped for refugee families. Now, with the backlog we've gotten lately, they're sleeping all over the place. When everything works right, they're here for less than forty-eight hours before their destination plan is complete and our transport teams pick them up and take them on their way. We think of this more as a safe house. A place to catch your breath before disappearing."

"So where do people go from here?"

"Can't tell you that. That's on a need-to-know basis. We only tell people where their individual destination is. I'll say this. We find new identities and new places for folks to live, in areas where people aren't interested in asking questions. Some people choose to stay and help us run the Network."

They pass into another hallway, where a dozen people stand in line holding plates. Several turn at the sound of Bruce's voice and smile warmly. "Actually, our biggest challenge isn't security. It's normal sanitation. We had to retrofit some of the vertical shafts for chemical toilets, then drill ventilation." They take their place at the end of the kitchen line. "For water, my son and I rigged up a reservoir in another shaft and ran a line out to a runoff channel on the face of the mountain. But maintaining all the systems with so many refugees coming in these days keeps us hopping."

They approach three folding tables laid out as a make-shift serving station, where three women sit before enormous steaming kettles, holding ladles. "The menu doesn't have much variety, but we try to keep it good. It's almost completely vegetarian — vegetables, soups, pasta, lots of breads. You've got to get your carbs up here. You'll notice one thing, though. In the mountains, everything tastes better."

Their plates loaded, they take seats along a long, crowded wooden table. Bruce looks over at John, who has listened quietly throughout. "We have a great library over on the northern side. Rachel will take you there. You can stay there as long as you want. But John, if you really want to do something fun, you can hang out with some of the Scouts. They'll be glad to start teaching you what they know. You may even be able to help out on sentry duty." He catches Vern's questioning look. "Up here, everybody pitches in. Now — as soon as I can this afternoon, I'll meet with my team and try to come up with some exit plans for you guys. I'll let you know, and then we'll get together. Okay?"

"Well, there's really only one option for me."

"What's that?"

"Obviously — I'm going back to Boulder; I'm going to

get my wife and daughter back."

To Vern's surprise, Bruce looks down, a mournful, almost pained expression crossing his face. "Vern, I understand why you want to do that. But ... I don't think that's such a good idea."

Disbelief begins to flood Vern's senses. "It's not an idea at all — I have no choice. I'm not going to just traipse off into the wild blue yonder and leave the rest of my family behind."

"Vern, last month we had a man try exactly that. We went along; we even drove him back to Fort Collins so he could get his teenaged son out of a county facility. Before he'd been back three hours, he was arrested along with two of my volunteers. Brought up on state charges of evasion, resisting arrest, criminal conspiracy. See, the state police knows we exist. And they're trying desperately to find us. So when you disappear and they conclude you're with us, they place full surveillance on anyone and anything you care about. Without some of kind of professional extraction team, you stand no chance."

"Fine! Then let's put together an extraction team!"

"Good luck doing it. I'm sorry, but I won't volunteer any of my people to do it. You have to understand, Vern. I've got three men right now cooling their heels in a county jail because I did it before. If any of the other Refugees want to help you, that's their prerogative. I won't stop them."

"Glad to hear it."

"Listen to me, Vern. If you stay at large, at least there's a chance your family members can shake loose and come find us. But if you get caught and go to jail, your chances at reuniting fall to nothing. Your kids get put into the system. They'll be gone forever."

Vern rubs his eyes, frustration pouring over him in waves.

"Don't misunderstand me," Bruce continues, his voice

plaintive for the first time. "It's a horrible choice. It's a tragedy. But don't compound the tragedy by making a mistake. Your son is here with you. You leave him and go back, and he may never see you again."

"I thought you'd help me get them back," Vern replies, his head swimming, his mind somehow removing itself from this conversation. "That's why I came here."

"I'm sorry."

Bruce stands and extends a large hand. "We'll talk about this some more, okay? I'll come find you and we'll set up a conference. Right now, I really have to go. I'm sorry." And with a sudden turn he is off again, an adviser's hand upon his shoulder for a hurried conference as they walk away.

Vern takes a deep breath and looks around at their eating companions. "You okay?" he asks John.

"Yeah. This place is kinda fun. Like a secret hideout." Then he looks to his father, eyes wide. "Are we gonna leave Mom and Heather behind?"

The three dozen Refugees and support crew line the walls of the Common Room, crowd the floor, stand shoulder-to-shoulder. They also fill the hollowed cave with sound; a young man with a clerical collar strums a guitar enthusiastically, singing camp songs in a high voice, trying hard to brighten the Refugees' somber demeanors. And it happens: as the old tunes fill the room, their eyes dim and they remember other days. It seems to strike everyone that if they can enjoy each other here, in straits such as these, then perhaps the good old days will indeed return.

Bruce rises, a wry, almost bashful smile creasing his face. "Well, as most of you have heard by now, the people we've been praying for are actually here: Vern and John Yates from Boulder." All eyes turn to the two, then the whole room breaks into applause. Vern feels the warmth envelop him. They are fellow sufferers, partakers in a common fate. He almost feels he could break into tears; he rubs his eyes vigorously to avoid it. "Thank you," he says, mouthing almost soundlessly.

"See, Vern," Bruce continues, "we had no idea if you were headed our way, or if you even knew of the Network. But we've heard your story. We've read accounts in the newspaper about you and your wife and daughter. And we've asked God to lead you to us."

He then whirls back around to the others in an almost military about-face. "Folks, Vern and John need our prayers more than ever. Because half of his family is still behind in Boulder, he has a decision to make. Vern feels very strongly that he should go back and try to free his wife and daughter, even though he risks getting caught and imprisoned in the process. Or he can stay on the run, and hope and pray that somehow they'll be freed." He turns back to meet Vern's gaze with a piercing look. "It's a cruel dilemma. Some of the people in this room have faced it. I hope you'll let them be there for you."

Vern nods slowly, and the weight of the decision descends upon him like a physical burden.

Arms loaded high with blankets, Tom leads them to a secluded alcove in the mine shaft where an inflatable mattress awaits. "The biggest problem around here is the dust," he says, glancing over at the craggy walls around them. "I recommend taking off your shoes before you reach your bed. Walk on some of these old blankets here. These new ones," he stops to fling some thin, brightly colored blankets onto the mattress, "are a special high-tech fiber. You'll only need two."

He leaves them to their fatigue. They arrange the blankets, settle their backpacks along the wall.

Slowly, almost ceremoniously, father and son begin to remove the stiff and dingy clothing they have worn since the first day of their descent into chaos. Vern looks down for a spot to lay his denim shirt, and sees something on his boy's arm. He reaches forward and softly grazes a deep purple bruise, just above John's elbow. John does not flinch.

"When did that happen?"

"You remember," John answers. "That time when I started to fall over on that steep trail, and I bumped into the branch so hard."

"Oh." Just now he has heard something totally new in the boy's voice. Maybe it's been there all along, these past two weeks. Maybe it has taken their new surroundings to jar his awareness, make the change noticeable. Some tone of self-assurance, some depth of confidence that resonates somehow in his words. His boy has weathered a grueling experience well. He thinks about the strong and self-assured man his son will someday become. He feels a father's pride well up, then his eyes moisten.

"Dad," John says with a quick laugh, looking at him, "you look like you got beat up!"

He looks down. The boy is right: all along the length of his body lies a red explosion of welts, small cuts, abrasions and bruises. His stomach begins to constrict in an odd rhythm and he realizes he is laughing, loudly, right along with his son. How long has it been?

"You better watch it or I'll give you a bath!" he says between breaths. John smiles, raises an armpit, leans towards it and makes a face. Vern does the same and their laughter explodes again. They joked many times about their respective aromas, back before their noses became deadened to the hygienic sacrifices of fugitive life.

For a second, before the laughter begins to subside, Vern forgets that he is the boy's father. The sense of responsibility and paternal scrutiny evaporates and John becomes simply a friend, one with whom he has shared the most harrowing period of his life. And now, as it comes to an end, he and his companion share a heartfelt, liberating belly laugh, completely satisfying, completely at odds with their present situation.

Finally, they lie down on the mattress and pull the blankets over themselves. Within ten minutes, they are both asleep — their deepest, most satisfying slumber in a long time.

If anybody had told me five years ago that all these things would happen to me, I would have called them paranoid. I would have told them America is a reasonable place, that wild, oppressive scenarios do not happen here. People do not get persecuted in America.

Let's see ... how many historical periods would that have overlooked ... slavery ... Asian Americans during World War II ... Wounded Knee ... the Mormon persecutions ... the civil rights struggles ...

No, I would have glossed over those things. I would have said America was too educated, too sophisticated to let a productive, respectable portion of its population be systematically harassed. But what about Bosnia? Russia? Nazi Germany? Weren't they modern, educated societies?

I've gotta face it. I just didn't want to look at the reality — even when there was still time to change it.

It was just arrogance. I figured America was magically immune from the kinds of abuses being committed in Europe and throughout the world. But I never looked at how they started. Media bias. "Anything goes" attitudes. Scapegoating. A wholesale loss of moral restraint. Machiavellian political strategies.

I didn't look to see that they were taking root right here, too. Right under my nose ...

1989. *Homosexuals invade mass at New York City's St. Patrick's Cathedral, shouting obscenities, throwing condoms and defiling Communion elements.*

1991. *A Minneapolis Catholic Archdiocese is fined $15,000 and assessed $20,000 in damages after homosexuals complain the church denied them their "right" to meet in church-owned facilities.*

1991. *Gay demonstrators dressed in suits and ties infiltrate a brunch at First Baptist Church of Atlanta, then suddenly pepper the diners with hundreds of condoms, and chant, "Safer sex saves lives!"*

1992. *The Attorney General of Hawaii rules that, under a state "gay rights" law, church leaders are legally required to consider homosexuals for all church positions except the pastorate itself.*

1992. *A New Jersey "gay rights" law prohibits all employers, including churches, from discriminating on the basis of "sexual orientation," requiring churches to marry homosexuals. The measure is overturned thanks to outraged conservatives.*

1994. *In Sweden, an evangelical pastor is jailed for preaching a sermon from Romans 1 ruled to be "belittling" to homosexuals.*

ELEVEN

What an appropriate place for me. A hole in the ground. Dark, cold, forgotten.

Vern lays disconsolate against an old mattress propped against the dirt in a pitiable attempt at comfort. Off in the darkness, laughter betrays the camaraderie of Johnny playing with a Scout friend. He can see their shapes against the round light of the far-off mine entrance, slapping, punching playfully. It's amazing, he thinks, how quickly children adapt. How quickly they can forget the grimmest realities.

He, however, cannot forget. During the long days of his escape he had imagined that finding Refuge would erase the uncertainty, solve his dilemma. Other people would know what to do, and immediately set him on his course. He had never imagined that his case would prove so unusual, that the decision would be so entirely his own to make. He never dreamed that redemption would require him to retrace his steps alone, unravel the ground he had gained, and simply sneak back to the city of his waking nightmares to restore his shattered family.

Right now he would like nothing better than to dig a little deeper into this hard earth and sleep. A long, oblivious slumber.

Somewhere in the darkness, he hears a door creak open, then shut. Advancing towards him through pools of light come fleeting glimpses of a visitor. A man. Then, suddenly, a face high above becomes visible as it bends down towards him.

"Hi, Vern. Mind if I sit down?"

He recognizes the earnest voice of Brent, the young guitar-playing pastor. The lanky frame bends and with an exhaled breath the visitor sits and leans back.

"Not trying to be nosy — but I hear you're kinda having a hard time of it."

"Yeah, you could say that."

"Feel like talking?"

"Not really. I feel like I'm in an impossible situation, that's all."

"I understand. When I first came here, I got seriously depressed. Not just the darkness and the discomfort, but ... I just felt sorry for myself. It seemed like my life wasn't worth living anymore. And you know what helped?" A pause — Brent seems to want him to ask. Vern waits for the man to answer himself.

"I'll tell you what. I started talking to the people around me. Pretty soon I found out I didn't have it so bad. There's a lot of stories in this place that're tough to beat. Most everybody here's been through stuff that's almost unthinkable."

He leans forward and looks for Vern's gaze. "I'm serious. You oughta try it. It'll make you feel better."

"All right. Let's start with you."

"Fair enough. My story's probably not the worst, but it'll give you an idea." Brent leans back a little further and stares up into the old logs lining the ceiling.

◆ ◆ ◆

I'm not sure where to start. First of all, I can sure say I didn't go to seminary to become some kind of fugitive activist. I was called to minister to people, to share with them the Good News that God had made a way out of their sins. I still do.

But I started hearing rumors a few years ago.

First I read that Canada had made it a crime to say anything critical of homosexuality over the radio. Twenty-five thousand dollar fine for airing those kinds of beliefs. I called up a Canadian friend, and he confirmed it was true. I thought about radio evangelists up there, prohibited from reading whole sections of the Bible. And it hits me — Canada is no third-world banana republic. It's our sister country, and if that can happen there ...

It worried me, but I put it out of my mind. Hasn't happened in my backyard yet, I told myself.

Then in 1991, this guy at a pastors' luncheon mentioned this new state proposal, this Ethnic Harassment Bill, proposed by Wilma Webb and supported by the whole state civil-rights establishment. He said it would make it a crime to speak out against homosexuality. If you said something that caused a homosexual to feel angry or hurt or offended, you were a felon. A hate criminal. Triple penalties and fines.

That law was shot down, and I thought, See, these things won't happen here.

When they finally passed the Hate Speech Law all those years later, part of me wasn't surprised. I didn't like it, but I figured it only regulated things that folks said to each other out on the street, in conversations out in public.

So the day came when I knew it was time to address homosexuality from the pulpit. I don't know how they got the word. Maybe at the shop where our bulletins got printed — I don't know. The sermon title was plain enough in the Order of Service. The Homosexuality Question: a Righteous and Compassionate Response. All I know is that Sunday morning, there sat two rows of people dressed for war. Leather jackets, leather boots, pierced noses, lips, t-shirts with gay slogans. Everybody in the congregation was petrified, but I figured this was my chance to minister to some people I might never speak to again.

So I picked up my Bible and read the chosen passage. Romans One ...

"For they exchanged the truth of God for a lie, and worshiped and served the creature rather than the Creator, who is blessed forever. Amen.

"For this reason God gave them over to degrading passions, for their women exchanged the natural function for that which is unnatural, and in the same way also the men abandoned the natural function of the woman and burned in their desire for one another, men with men committing indecent acts and receiving in their own persons the due penalty of their error."

And you know something? I wasn't going to stand there and damn those people. I wasn't going to condemn them and thump my Bible in their faces. I was going to tell them that God offered them forgiveness. And freedom. And true love that would really satisfy. I was going to explain in a gentle way that the reason they felt so much anger and fear and self-loathing was because they were in bondage, and despite what the world told them, there was a way out.

I would have told them all those things. It was all there in my message outline, ready to be said.

But while I read the passage I started hearing hissing. It got louder and louder, and pretty soon out of the corner of my eye I saw that two of them were standing and had put whistles to their mouths. By the time I'd finished reading, condoms were flying across the sanctuary.

One girl yanked up a tank top and exposed her breasts. I mean, there were children in there, we don't dismiss for children's service until right before the offertory ...

Then they left. Several of the ushers were starting to roughhouse a few of them, and they just gave a signal, turned around and ran out. We spent the rest of the morning in a kind of impromptu prayer service. Just trying to overcome our anger and pray for them.

I thought that was bad enough. But the next morning, a police car pulled up. An officer rang at my door and said I was under arrest for a hate crime.

You know something? I laughed in his face. I know it wasn't a smart thing to do, but the thought that I had committed a crime against those people was so ludicrous that I couldn't help it. It seemed so unreal; even when I felt the handcuffs snap around my wrist, it just felt like some weird skit or a bad TV movie.

It was no joke. One of the lesbian girls sat in the station lobby, crying and acting all upset. I had caused her "trauma," she said. I had seen her laughing and hissing with all the rest, yet her story now was that I had inflicted this psychological wound that would take her months of therapy and years of nightmares to overcome.

I think the police even knew she was a complete fake. But they had no choice — they enforce the laws we pass ...

I was sentenced to six months probation and ordered to attend a "sensitivity training" class that would cost me $400. I told the judge I would not attend because the nature of the course material constituted an infringement on my freedom of belief. The judge threw me in jail.

My third week there, our church was firebombed. It burned to the ground. I got out six days later, and there was no church for me to pastor. My congregation was too scared to gather again. I started holding Bible studies in members' living rooms, but people were too scared to have me seen at their houses, what with the continuing death threats and the police and all. So I had to go out and get another job.

When I heard about the Refuge, I really felt like God was calling me here. It may be a cold mine in the middle of nowhere, but I'm ministering again. And that's all that matters.

It is what passes for nighttime in the mine, the lighting reduced to one red bulb per passage, the crowded row of sleeping humanity strangely quiet except for an occasional echoing snore and the hissing of the space heaters.

Vern walks over and sits beside a sleepless middle-aged woman, huddled in a blanket. She smiles at him, a weak grin filtered through a haze of grief and shock. He turns towards her; her hand leaves the blanket for a handshake. "Myrna Rosemond. I'm from Greeley."

"Vern Yates." She smiles again, stronger this time. Vern nods yes, his eyes still closed.

"I guess they told you about the backlog," she whispers, lamely trying to spur a conversation. He nods again. "It's amazing. When I first got here, there were only a half dozen people. Now look at it. I hear they're even refitting more mine shafts over on the Divide, north of here."

"It *is* amazing. This many people on the run ... I just keep wondering how we let all this happen."

"I don't know either. I know for myself, I didn't see it until it was right in front of me. You remember when Congress passed that bill? Employment-nondiscrimination, something like that. It sounded good. My husband and I, we owned a little copy shop, we always said we were against discrimination. We didn't care about our employees being gay."

So, two days after the law passed, this employee of ours showed up wearing a T-shirt that showed two men french kissing each other. He wouldn't take it off. We could tell it horrified our customers. Then, to punish us for asking, he wore it two days straight. So, my husband fired him. Had no choice.

A week later we got the subpoena. Discrimination lawsuit.

My husband didn't hate anybody. Never had. But in court the judge told Carl he was a "rank homophobe" on the basis of being personally opposed to homosexuality. The judge said Carl had tried to censor his employee's free expression. He said free expression was the essence of the kid's "sexual orientation."

Carl was taking it all okay, right up until the auctioneers came for our inventory and the boards went over the windows. Our whole life savings had gone into building that business. Then the next day, this police car pulls into my driveway. The officer comes in, sits on my couch — just like that, tells me my husband's been found at a rest stop off Interstate 25 with a bullet through his forehead and a revolver in his hand.

It's a mess, I'm telling you. I, for one, never thought it would come to this. I thought all the gays wanted was equal rights. Like everybody else wants, I guess. And then I thought they'd go away.

The victor will never be asked if he told the truth.

Adolf Hitler, *Mein Kampf,* 1929.

I have helped to create a truly fascist organization ... We conspired to bring into existence an activist group that ... could effectively exploit the media for its own ends, and would work covertly and break the law with impunity ... we subscribed to consciously subversive modes, drawn largely from the voluminous Mein Kampf, *which some of us studied as a working model. As ACT-UP/D.C. grew, we struck intently and surgically into whatever institution we believed to stand in our way ...*

Eric Pollard, co-founder of the Washington D.C. chapter of the militant gay group ACT-UP, 1991.

TWELVE

Oddly, it seems to help a little. He feels almost buoyed by the knowledge that his is not the most woeful tale in this place. Embarrassed, yet also resigned to this perverse task of coaxing out the disintegration of people's lives, he begins walking around to various chambers, striking up conversations.

He finds Ken reading a book by the glow of a small penlight.

"Mind if I interrupt?"

A pause, while Ken puts down his book, clicks off the light, looks over to him. "No. I don't mind."

"I just was curious about how you ended up here."

"I don't understand. How ..."

"Just ... your story. What happened to you. I'm kind of putting the bigger picture together."

"Oh. Well, it starts a long time ago." He begins absently rubbing patterns in the soft dirt with his palm. He stops, dusts his hand off. "I spent three years in the lifestyle." He pauses, accustomed to the thirty seconds or so people usually need to acquaint themselves with the idea. "I just — it's hard to say why, other than the typical patterns about the same-sex parent and all that. Anyway, I

103

became convinced sometime in my late teens that this was the answer to my unhappiness, so I came out of the closet, dropped out of school, and moved to Denver."

And let me tell you something. I was never more miserable than those years I spent "in the life."

Of course, I had a whole nationwide movement to tell me this was normal, I was just suffering from "internalized homophobia," that with time and wisdom and maybe some therapy I'd get over it. It was my parents' fault. After all, they were Christians. Enough said.

Looking back on it now, I realize that an awful lot of energy was being spent trying to keep me in the lifestyle, to keep me convinced that this was the only right course for my life.

I could come in, but they'd make it as tough as possible to get out.

So for several years I lived the life of a young, urban gay man. Dancing at clubs every night possible. Working as a waiter, working out at the gym every chance I got. Drifting in and out of sexual relationships, usually lasting only a few weeks. And throughout, visiting bathhouses on the side to spice things up, get some of the "action" everybody told me I was entitled to.

I added it up, once. In about three years, I had sex with about 175 different men. Back then, I was proud of this.

I got the usual diseases, the typical laundry list of sexually transmitted viruses and illnesses and syndromes. And then one day I tested for HIV. Two weeks later someone called me at home and asked me to come in to the clinic.

"You're positive," the doctor told me. That word, "positive," sounded so funny, like this person was telling me I had a sunny outlook on life or something. Instead of precisely the opposite, that my life was going to end horribly. When I heard those words, everything came crashing

down — all the slogans and manifestoes and clichés about my sexuality, all the lies I'd believed about myself. I realized that I had been duped.

Leaving "the life" was really difficult, though, because it became obvious real quick that my whole existence had been constructed around being gay. All my friends were gay. My neighborhood was gay. Nearly everybody I worked with was gay. My wardrobe, my books, my whole identity was built on my sexuality. And then it hit me — here was more proof of how hard I had been working to make myself accept the lies. I was no average, ordinary American who "just so happened" to have this tiny little deviation from the norm. Every cell in my body was working overtime to be as gay as possible, and feel really, really good about it.

So I started attending a church every so often, kinda slipping in the back door real discreetly. I started trying to pray, to tell God that I hadn't forgotten Him, and that I was ready to accept the truth for a change.

And one Sunday the pastor said they were starting a support ministry for people who were in conflict with their homosexuality and wanted to leave the lifestyle. So I went, and I met a whole roomful of people who felt exactly like I did. They knew they were in for the fight of their lives, that they'd gotten trapped in one of the most powerful addictions you can ever fall into. But they were determined to become whole again. They were totally committed to turning their sexuality over to the Creator.

One night I came home from the group, and my house was filled with about thirty people — gay and lesbian friends and lovers, ex-lovers and employers from my past, all there together, just about choking out the whole space. It was an intervention, they said. One by one they took turns telling me that I'd fallen into a cult, that I was being brainwashed into denying my sexuality, that I had to come back to my senses and just work a little harder on accepting myself as God had made me.

It turned into a shouting match, because since in fact I

was not brainwashed, I had calm, rational answers for what they said. I tried to turn it into an opportunity to share with them some of what I had learned. But the harder I tried to communicate with them, the angrier and louder they became.

Finally, after two and a half hours, they gave up. Their hostility just spent itself and they all filed out, still fuming at me. I heard comments from them as they walked by like, "I wish we could deprogram him," or "It's those homophobic quacks. They oughta be locked up."

That night, I knew I'd turned a corner. But I also knew that the further I moved away from the old lifestyle, the more it was going to fight back.

A couple years went by, and pretty soon I was a facilitator myself. I had my own ex-gay ministry, and I was helping about a dozen other people who wanted out. That's when it really started getting vicious. The hard-core militants wanted ministries like mine stopped — no matter what. Persuasion didn't work, so their harassment escalated. Their direct action groups attacked our offices three times over an eight-month period. They threw paint on the walls. They phoned in death threats almost daily. One morning the Lesbian Avengers dumped jarfuls of locusts onto the carpet, and climbed on our desks, stomping and screaming.

And when that didn't work, they started pulling power plays.

For years, the gay political activists had been working on turning the psychological establishment completely against us. Back in '73, they had bullied the American Psychological Association into taking homosexuality off the DSM list of mental disorders, even though most of the membership disagreed. But that wasn't enough. In my fourth year of ministry they got a committee to pass a resolution declaring that it was "unethical" to conduct an ex-gay ministry.

A couple years ago they listed homophobia as a mental illness, something they'd been talking about for years.

Now, I know some people I would call homophobic. They can't talk to a gay person, they leave if one enters the room — they can't interact or treat them like another human being. They have no problem talking to an alcoholic, someone with a more acceptable addiction. They really do have a phobia about homosexuality.

But you and I know that the word has a far broader meaning these days. Anybody who disagrees with even the smallest little item in the gay agenda is a "homophobe." Anybody who doesn't feel it's entirely natural to commit anal intercourse, for instance, is now considered crazy.

Pretty soon my liability insurance had tripled. I knew I wouldn't be able to keep the group going for long. But they took care of that for me — the Department of Health ordered me to cease and desist. I was performing "unsafe" and "untherapeutic" practices.

You know, for the longest time I'd thought ill of the conservatives trying to oppose gay rights. I'd thought they were my biggest enemies. That they were part of the true homophobic contingent. That they needed to get a life.

Pretty soon my life was destroyed. And I turned into an activist. Despite myself.

You have to understand that the motivations of the gay community are validation. They want to be approved. They want people to say, 'It's okay that you're gay.' So basically the gay community is trying to turn the world into a 12-step gay support group, trying to get everyone out there to be a member ... and if you disagree with one tiny, insignificant little point of their wide, broad, sweeping agenda, you're all of a sudden a homophobe and a hatemonger. You're a villain. A bad guy. And this is ludicrous.

Luke Montgomery, once known as the notorious and flamboyant gay militant "Luke Sissyfag," today profoundly disillusioned with the "community" he once embraced.

THIRTEEN

Hal, a young black man in his early twenties, swallows hard when Vern asks him his story, casually, over a lunch of ramen soup and bread. The ordeal is not one he is accustomed to revisiting. "It's pretty simple, really. I was a graduate student at C.U., and I needed a roommate to help make ends meet. So I put an ad in the paper."

The first guy who answered the ad was perfect. Cleancut, had a good job, said he didn't party a whole lot. We talked for almost an hour and I was about to say yes, when he cleared his throat, looked down at the floor and told me he was gay. Then he looked up at me, real funny, like he was just waiting for my response. I don't know if he was expecting a fight, or what.

I told him real politely that I was uncomfortable with it, and that based on that, it probably wouldn't be a good idea. The guy just shook his head like he was a little disappointed. He said, "Sorry I've wasted your time." A little sarcastically, I guess. But I didn't expect anything major to come of it. I mean, there's no shortage of places to live in Boulder for people who can afford them.

But apparently, he did mind. He went and filed a complaint with the city.

Three days later the police showed up and took me in to the police station. At first I couldn't believe it. I mean, isn't there something called freedom of association? Aren't we supposed to be able to choose the people we live with and hang out with, in this country?

I just kept shaking my head, like the whole thing was a bad dream. They questioned me for three hours. Asked me all sorts of questions about my beliefs. Did I hate gays? Did I belong to all sorts of extremist organizations who had filled my head with propaganda against diverse people?

The judge leveled a fine against me for fifteen hundred dollars, which I couldn't afford to pay. He told me if I didn't pay it within three days he'd throw me in County Correctional for thirty days. He told me to report to the local gay group for sensitivity training, for which I would pay $250. He told me to report back to the court six months later for a review of my rental decisions.

I felt like I was living in Cuba or something. So I did what the Cubans do.

I took off for parts unknown.

The all clear sounds and several dozen refugees emerge single file from the center of the mountain and onto a shallow bowl along its eastern slope. The mine's auxiliary shaft leads out to a small, high valley, sheltered by the sheer rock walls of the Apostles, and at its center, a tiny lake, glowing softly with the last light of the dying day.

On quiet nights when the Scouts have verified the absence of hikers along busy Clear Creek to the West, the refugees allow themselves this luxury of fresh air and walks along the water's edge. For the first few minutes they only stand straight and stretch their limbs, crane their heads and gaze eagerly into the blue glow of a cool, moonlit evening.

Vern whispers a word of caution to his son and watches him scramble down toward the water with two Scouts, their voices floating back to him in small excited fragments. Spotting a piece of crumbling granite, he sits down to try and quiet his thoughts.

Why, he thinks, did it take him this long to come to his senses? It's not that he hasn't loved his family. He had just always thought family was part of the package of ordinary life. Standard equipment. He tries to picture a future life without all of them together. He imagines Johnny walking into some melancholy home thick with memories of an absent mother, ringing with the awful silence of a little girl's absent voice. One thing he knows for sure. It's not a life he can live with.

"Good kid," says a deep male voice beside him.

Vern turns to see the bearded face of someone he knows only as Jim, a good-natured man in his early fifties. His eyes are fixed on Johnny, and filled with tears. "Yeah, he sure is," Vern answers. "We've been through a lot together."

The man digs into the mountain with a pocket knife, hard. Just stabbing the blade into the rocks. His face looks as if he has just swallowed something deeply bitter.

"You have any children?" Vern asks.

Jim looks up vaguely, as if the pain written on his features is somewhere above Vern's head. "Yeah. I have a son of my own."

Karen and I had him later, in our late thirties. Our only son. Truly the light of our lives, the apple of our eye. Bright, articulate, precocious even. Good-looking kid, always.

He started having the problems in junior high, but they seemed kind of typical. Rebellion. Talking back. Grades dropped. His eighth grade year we scheduled a meeting and

*went in to talk with his school counselor, and he said every-
thing was okay, Gavin was seeing him and they were
working through things. He couldn't tell us anymore than
that because of confidentiality, which struck us as a little
odd, but we went along with it. Seemed like our boy was in
capable hands.*

*I remember driving home, Karen said that something
didn't seem quite right with the guy. Something — she
couldn't put her finger on it.*

*The counselor called back two weeks later and sched-
uled another meeting. This time, everything was different:
two of his teachers were sitting there, the school's attorney,
a vice-principal, all with serious game faces on. You could
cut the tension with a chainsaw.*

*The vice-principal started things off by telling us, "Mr.
and Mrs. Macy, we have some very important news to tell
you."*

*The counselor looked us and said, just like that, "Your
son is gay."*

*And I lost it. I'm not sure what I said, but I know I got
out of my seat and raised my voice. Karen kept trying to
yank me back into the chair, but I wouldn't sit down. I
wouldn't shut up. The thought of these people, these public
servants who act like the right hand of God, telling me my
son was a homosexual ...*

*Apparently my performance didn't go so well. By the time
I settled down, the counselor wouldn't meet my eye. He
coughed a couple of times and said, "Well, Gavin certainly
told us he lived in a highly homophobic environment."*

*They announced that Gavin was going to start attend-
ing an after-school program called Project 10, which was
essential for his mental health. A group for high-schoolers
who are "coming to terms with their orientation," to help
them accept themselves as they are, to help them come out of
the closet, to help cure them of the homophobia that has
infected them and endangered their psyches.*

So, they told us, we were legally required to let him

attend. We were even required to drive him, pick him up from this program. I told them, no way. No way are you ordering me to aid and abet in brainwashing my own child into a life-styles I disagree with with every bone in my body!

And they stayed very calm, and told me if I didn't do it, I would be charged with criminal neglect. And just like that, the meeting was over.

So I made a decision. The next day, we held Gavin back from school. We told him — and the counselor — that Karen and I were going to homeschool him. They said we couldn't do that. They told us Gavin was fighting suicidal tendencies, and that denying him the Project 10 support would seriously endanger his life.

I told him that Gavin would go back to a pro-homosexual youth group over my dead body.

And he told me that, from jail, my dead body wouldn't stop anything. Department of Social Services took him from our home two days later. With police escort. They took him to a so-called "gay friendly" home for youth. And a judge ordered us to pay child support for Gavin to stay there.

He was fifteen. I remember that fifteen for me was a real confusing time sexually — I didn't know which end was up, who I was, how I was supposed to behave. What if I had gone to my school counselor and been told I might be gay? I mean, how many kids are genuinely confused and getting this kind of information?

The last time I saw my son, I hardly recognized him. The visit was supervised. They warned me not to make any negative statements. Gavin had purple hair and a ring through his nose. And he told us he had a boyfriend. He told us he was still HIV-negative, and that was a miracle, and couldn't we be happy for that, at least?

After that I refused to pay. It wasn't that I wanted to abandon my son, but I just couldn't contribute to that anymore. I had reached my limit. The home came after me. A judge ordered my salary docked automatically, and then sentenced me to a modified house arrest. I could go to work, then come home immediately. They put a collar on my ankle to make sure I didn't stray.

All because I wanted to raise my son according to his family's values. Karen and I divorced. The strain was too much. And with her gone, I just lost it. I dropped out. I came here.

He hears his next story the following morning, peeling potatoes with the kitchen detail near the half light of the tunnel entrance. A thick man, tanned and burly with the odd muscles of a construction worker, Frank focuses his pale blue eyes suddenly into Vern's. Apparently they see enough to invite candor, for he looks down and the eyes begin to flash with alternating blazes of grief and rage.

"It's a short story, really." He isn't looking at Vern now, but studying his potato as if a great secret were carved upon its knobby skin. "Tommy, you met him. He's my grandson. He and his five-year-old brother Brian lived with us since their parents, our daughter and her husband, split up. One day I'm late picking Brian up from Scouts. Everyone else is gone and since I feel bad for being late I just barge right in. And there ..."

His voice breaks; for a second he sounds like a boy just hitting puberty.

"And there..."

He looks at Vern as if to show him the tears, but of course Vern knows they're there, and he turns back. "And there's the Scoutmaster, performing, you know, oral ... sex, on the boy."

He has dropped the pretense of peeling the potato now; the yellow lump hangs from his hand. He stares at the ground, shaking his head as if he will never stop.

"I beat the living spit outta him. Put him in the hospital with a broken jaw, busted cheekbone, nose, three teeth missing. And when he got out he sued me and the Young Scouts both."

He looks back to Vern. "He took my house and my retirement money. I got nothing left to live for now, except those two boys. I'd gladly die if it gave me the chance to put a bullet right between that man's eyes."

He seems to need Vern's agreement that yes, in fact, he looks like he would. "I've told these folks running this place, they got a nice setup, but it's not enough. Hidin' in the hills isn't gonna cut it. This is war, and we gotta fight it like a war. That's why we're losing. You hear what I'm saying?"

Vern nods, if only to hear where Frank is headed.

"Some of us up here have got a plan. An alternate plan from Bruce and his nice boys. We're gonna take the war down to the enemy."

"But how can you possibly win against the U.S. government?"

"Same way the Viet Cong did. Attrition. Strike and withdraw. Guerilla war."

"And what are you going to accomplish?"

"We're going to never let them forget, that's what. We'll make them remember what they've done to us and our kids. We're gonna make a stand."

Vern thinks about it. "I don't want to make a stand," he tells him, straight and level. "I just want my family back."

In the days that follow, Vern finds out that Frank is the only person there who has ever done anything against a homosexual — yelled an insult, inflicted harm, even made a threat.

For the rest of them, their beliefs have brought them to this place, made them what they are.

Criminals.

And yes, hearing their stories does bring him around to the urgency of his one saving knowledge — that all is not lost, his wife is waiting for him, his daughter can be found if he tries. At least his relatives are alive and united in spirit.

He can save his family — if he'll just find a way.

Each passing day grows warmer in the Sawatch range, and this day is no exception. Scattered across the alpine tundra, the Refugees take a sunshine break out on the hidden side of the mountain.

A soft motion flutters in his peripheral vision and before Vern knows it Frank is crouching beside him, lighting a pipe. His eyes focus on the mountains ahead, not meeting Vern's, but a cagey squint makes it clear the man has something to say. "So Vern, you give any thought to what I told you?"

"I didn't know ... were you proposing something?"

Frank seems irritated at that response. "Yeah. I was. We all heard they don't know what to do with you. I understand why, but that doesn't help you any. You're not an operational guy — you got no idea what action to take."

"You're right about that."

"So what I'm telling you is, maybe your solution is to take up arms against your oppressor."

It's Vern's turn now to gaze out at the mountains without a word. Something about this doesn't feel right. The man, the attitude. His churning gut would love for him to blow a few folks away, but somehow ... He wishes Frank would leave, let him think in peace. He turns.

"I hear what you're saying. I'm going to think about it."

"You do that."

God, I never knew how much my family meant to me until today. I'm so sorry. You know I love them dearly. But I never realized what it would feel like to have us separated

like this. It feels like a part of my chest has been ripped out from me. Like I'm walking around with this giant hole through the middle of my soul.

Forgive me for thinking of Gail and John and Heather like they were some kind of trophy. I forgot what life used to be like without them.

Are they all right, God? Are you watching over my wife and daughter? Only you know how much I worry about them. I should be there. I should be protecting them, comforting them, making a way for us to stay together.

God, if you'll return my family to me, I'll never take them for granted again. Just, please. Help me bring us back together again.

Please?

Vern dreams of a real moment in his childhood. The living room is exactly as it was, his father young and thin, precisely as he had looked in his late thirties. The dream replays it perfectly. He'd climbed up on his father's knee to ask him about Korea.

"What did you do in the war, Daddy? Tell me ... what did you do in the war?"

1989. *Anne Ready and Maureen Rowe of Madison, Wisconsin advertise for a third roommate. When a lesbian answers, Ann replies, "No thanks." The lesbian files a discrimination complaint.*

Ann and Maureen are summoned before Madison's Equal Opportunity Commission. They are interrogated for hours, ordered to pay thousands in damages, to write a letter of apology, to have their rental decisions monitored for the next two years, and to attend "sensitivity training" at a local homosexual organization. The commission rules that their personal objections to homosexuality are invalid. Pleading that this would bankrupt them, they are told, "That's not our problem." The commission rules they lost their right to privacy when they entered the public marketplace.

In 1992, after three years, enormous public outcry and a $10,000 legal tab, the Madison City Council drops the penalties.

FOURTEEN

Metal cross over a plunging roof. White paneled walls. Painted windows. Glassed-in sign: "Fraser Baptist Assembly. Sunday School 9:30 a.m. Service 11:00 a.m.. Christ worshipped here."

Yeah right, she thinks with a small laugh. Christ worshipped here along with hatred, bigotry, patriarchal domination, Judeo-Christian cultural imperialism, fear of the unknown ... at least a dozen other fascist creeds she could name in a heartbeat.

Sonya sits still in the car seat and lets the queasy knot in her stomach slowly untie itself. Even after all these months it happens nearly every time, staking out these little evangelical hovels. Sit by the hour staring at one of those places, it puts a different perspective on things. She'll describe it all to her lesbian sisters later, back in the coffeehouses of Denver. Everyone shudders with those sympathetic grimaces reserved for martyrs. *You just sit there and stare at 'em?*

Got to. Only way to catch the bigots in the act.

The narrow building with its narrow windows brings back all those starched and sterile Sundays of her youth in Texas. Musty Sunday school rooms, tiny chairs stacked in corners, the odor of soiled diapers and inadequate

119

disinfectant Walls bare, except for the posters and their exhortations to righteousness.

"The devil trembles when he sees — the weakest sinner on his knees."

"Dance to a beat, you dance with the devil."

"Lose your soul to rock n' roll."

And always the women carrying potluck dishes, foil stretched tight over glass bowls. Some sort of casserole always: chicken, tuna, taco, spaghetti. The free hand always holding a child — ever breeding brand new baby Christians for the nursery roll. Few smiles, except of course when the women passed each other in the bright linoleum hallways. But Sonya knew. She would watch their unguarded moments. She'd spot the truth on their faces, in lines and furrows around the eyes and mouths.

In college, years later, her professors had given her the explanation: the Christian women of her youth had simply been oppressed. Slaves of a male-dominated system, they had been held captive by insidious lies about "family roles" and the dictates of procreation.

She remembers the precise moment it had all fallen into place in her mind ... cross-legged in the breeze and the deep spring grass, a dozen girls beside that Female Studies professor with the warm, mellow voice that flowed so earnestly. Complete and inescapable, the realization had fallen into place, like a leaf falling from a vast, wise tree. *The only force holding this world back from a blissful future is the stranglehold of Judeo-Christian dogma.* The Crusades, the Inquisition, the Nazis, the Jim Crow South, the ravaged environment — it was all their fault. Those fanatics with their vengeful god, their guilt and rage. They've poisoned the human race long enough.

Her future had appeared before her, rich as a painting. *That's what I'll do with my life. I'll help rid the world of this cancer. We'll argue and we'll educate and we'll legislate, and then one day when the time is ripe, we'll get tough with the diseased remnants. Start the mop-up action. We'll cleanse the world, make it new and clean. Sweep away the last of the oppressors.*

Shortly afterwards, she took her first lover. After all the angry lectures about the enslavement of heterosexual couplings, after the countless stories of date rape and abusive men and the grotesque monstrosities of males in heat, it seemed the only right thing to do: sex with another woman. After all she'd heard, giving herself to a man would have seemed a casting of pearls before swine.

After months of insecurity, her consummation into the life-styles had all proven quite simple. Her own roommate. She cultivated the crush like a secret ember — long talks into the night, conversations deliberately steered to the insufficiencies of men and the innate longing of the female soul, followed by lingering back rubs and casual brushes of the hand. By the spring of her junior year it had erupted into a full-blown love affair, well-known up and down the dorm as one of the hottest lesbian trysts of that semester.

She doesn't dwell on the relationship too often, at least not its conclusion. At the end of the school year, her roommate had maddeningly deluded herself into believing she was straight after all, that their time of passion was just a fleeting experiment on the wild side of the libido. More likely, Sonya always tells herself, she couldn't bear the thought of going home for the summer to her lifeguard job and the constant task of facing down all the testosterone-ridden men of her hometown. And sure enough, the spineless girl had starting dating a man that summer, a man Sonya imagines as slick and convincing, a man who talked her lover into quitting college and marrying him and becoming his meek domestic subject. They had never spoken again. Sonya imagines with a bitter tug that her first lover has never told him of their relationship. She ruefully pictures her sitting at a window, longing for the long-ago joys of lesbian love. *Tough. You chose your life, you live it.*

It's usually a satisfying scenario, and today is no exception.

Sonya sits watching the church, savoring the sweet bile of the jilted.

Finally, her moment comes. At two o'clock in the afternoon, a pale brown Oldsmobile pulls into the pastor's parking spot and a balding young man steps out into the sun, carrying a battered briefcase.

She waits while he unlocks the door and closes it gently behind him. She counts off ten seconds. Now he'll be walking through a cramped hallway lined with flyers about summer camps and missionary appeals. One minute more and he'll enter some small office with rows of Bible commentaries and old shag underfoot. She waits until she locks on the image of him leaning back into a cracked vinyl desk chair. Then she steps out.

Striding across the pavement, she gets a feeling.

I'm an instrument of justice. A weapon of the state. The state always finds its man, and right now the state is me, right here closing in. No wasted time; no wasted energy. Nothing but this lean fire in my belly. The bigots are gonna pay. They're gonna pay for their years of hateful dominance over this culture. For every moment of misery a gay or lesbian ever suffered through.

The hallway is only slightly different than she'd imagined. One thing she can say about her job — she's gotten to know her church layout. She nudges past the open door without a knock and walks to the edge of his desk, savoring the purpose and strength in her stride. It makes her smile inside, even as her face hardens into a mask of hostile intensity.

He's actually praying, she realizes, as his head rises from the desktop and his hands unfold. Got a true believer here, actually doing it. He stands and just smiles at her, not even perturbed by the rude entrance, not even a shadow across the eyes. The smile goes clear through. Scary. She doesn't trust the unconflicted—they always make the worst fanatics.

"Pastor Dave," he says in a low voice, putting out his hand.

She takes it and squeezes hard. "Sonya," she says in her best low voice.

His brow creases with a question. Does he know her? "Glad to meet you ... Or have we met before at a service..."

"We've never met. I'm a born-again pagan, butch dyke, and proud of it. This isn't a social call."

She can barely stand the thought that he might, even for a second, have mistaken her for another of his sniveling penitents, one more co-dependent weakling come to beg his patronizing attentions and sloppy prayers. *Patch up my wounds, Pastor Dave. Send me off with an earnest platitude and a cheesy dollop of pop psychology. After I've left you can kick back, resume your easy life. Your comfortable, bourgeois existence, living off the guilt of others. You parasite ...*

She reaches in, pulls out her badge and flashes it in a practiced motion. "Fully deputized tracker for the State of Colorado, Mister Johnson." She loves calling him that, "mister," no titles. "So — shall we sit down?"

His eyes are roaming now, frantically scanning everything in the room. "Uhh, maybe I ought to have my attorney present."

"You have the right. But I'm in a hurry. Tell me what I want to know, and I'll recommend that the D.A. not prosecute." She sits down before he does and palms the armrest magisterially. "Make me wait, I might change my mind."

He looks around the room, uncertain. "What is it you want to know?"

"My sources tell me you helped out a couple of vagabonds who showed up here a while ago. Vernon and John Yates. I want to know where you transported them." He stares at her. She can almost see the churning in that fundamentalist brain, the dim mind battling fear paralysis. "Yates is a child abuser and a criminal fugitive, Mister Johnson. We know you aided and abetted him. And others. That's a felony."

His face begins to turn stony. Finally some anger. His

hand lifts, holding a phone receiver. He looks down and punches a number. While he waits he turns his back to her, fixing his eyes on a trash can in the far corner.

"Yeah Larry, Pastor Dave. I've got a ... tracker from the state here, threatening me with prosecution if I don't tell her things." He falls silent. Then he nods. "Okay. Thanks, Larry. I'll be in touch." He turns to her again. "You have no legal right. If I'm prosecuted I'll assert my rights under the Fifth Amendment. But right now, I have to ask you to leave."

"So, no Pastor Dave anymore, huh?"

"You're not looking to me as a pastor."

"That's right. I'm outta here. But the next knock on your door will be from the county sheriff."

She's almost out the door when he shifts, the tension leaving his body. "You know, as a pastor I can tell you that there's hope for you. You can leave the life-styles if you want."

"Oh, please."

"I'm serious. God didn't create you to be this way. He can help you break free."

Her head feels assaulted by the anger; she pictures her fist striking the man's smug face. "Stop it! Can't you shut off your propaganda for even a minute?"

"If you're talking about the gospel of Jesus, no."

She interrupts, jabbing her finger at him. "If you say another word, I'll arrest you right now." She turns away before he has a chance to speak — fanatic like that, he might keep on anyway. Just to be a martyr. Just then a piercing beep at her waist tells her she's being paged. Halfway out the door, she reaches back in with a pointed finger.

"Not a word."

The message is from Rusty with State Patrol — someone at Clear Creek Reservoir called in a tip about a man and a boy asking for food. Matched the descriptions.

This one's legitimate. South of Leadville. A wilderness area, right up against the Divide. Great excuse for a little more backpacking.

She drives west, up the interstate over Vail Pass, past the condos and snow lodges crowded in a garish display of capitalism gone mad. At Minturn she turns off and starts to climb over Tennessee Pass, a vast gorge plunging off beside her and beyond, the high places of the Holy Cross Wilderness.

Holy Cross? Why'd they have to call it that? The fanatics even made relics out of Mother Earth! Can't they leave her alone?

Sometimes she wonders if she's obsessed with these people. In her free moments she composes angry monologues to them in her head, slashing down their hoary lies with wild strokes of razor-sharp logic, pounding them with hammer blows of truth and reason and tolerance. She has an image in her head, as vivid as a blacklight poster, of the composite Aryan male Christian sexist homophobic meat-eating wife-abusing pig — a face glaring at her with dark, blow-dried hair, the florid and pockmarked complexion of a hillbilly, and a smug, superior grin ...

Her lovers tell her that sometimes she cries out in the night. She acts surprised but inside she knows why. She's screaming at that face.

The waiting deputy points her down the valley, in the direction the man and boy had headed. The fisherman had given them a bag of chips and a candy bar, said the two had been very polite and grateful, maybe too grateful. The next day, he'd seen the posters in Leadville.

She feels the road lead her like an artery farther into the heart of the wild. Now unpaved, it follows the creek past several crumbled mining settlements, and delivers her to a dilemma. At Winfield the valley splits — the map tells her North and South Clear Creek split towards diverging ridges. Then, with a smirk, she spots three words woven into the dotted line of the Divide.

The Three Apostles.

Wouldn't it be hilarious? The Christians never could leave it alone. Couldn't be that easy ...

She pitches her tent near the trailhead for the night. In the morning, she rises without breakfast and girds herself for a trek. Slipping past the gate and onto the trail, she thinks now only of her quarry. It's hard not to feel eyes watching her from the woods. They could be anywhere — there are only thirty million tree trunks for them to hide behind. Thankfully, they don't know her. She's just another backpacker. Although, she thinks with a chuckle, quite obviously a butch dyke.

Don't engage, they keep telling her in Denver. You're a tracker — you locate, call in coordinates, and let the Patrol do its job.

As the flat gives way to incline and her lungs work harder, her thoughts become more tortured and angry. She will not guess how much of her stamina the disease has already devoured, but in the back of her mind she feels her strength waning.

AIDS. The evil virus wouldn't be in there now, running up and down her veins wreaking havoc, if the homophobic government had done its job. Sometimes she wants to be angry at David, her bisexual buddy who had told her it was OK, he'd tested negative the week before, but it all gets twisted in her mind — she's a lesbian, she's not supposed to have sex with men, not supposed to want to, an odd aberration really, drunk and stupid with her token male friend after a wild party down in Lodo and even worse, no condoms on hand. It's too difficult sorting that picture out.

Easier than wading into all that confusing territory is to focus her rage on Uncle Sam. Pawn of the ruling class. Icon of lies. Murderer. Some Uncle, huh, can't even protect me from a tiny virus. Won't part with the money to give me a decent life.

She stops and bends over, puffing. The anger has jacked

up her heartrate and stolen her wind. Holding her knees, she tells herself that it's not really her body failing her— it's those Christians. Even from a distance they suck away her strength.

... [homosexuals] possess political power much greater than their numbers ... they devote this political power to achieving not merely a grudging social toleration, but full societal acceptance, of homosexuality.

Justice Antonin Scalia, dissenting opinion,
Evans v. Romer (the Amendment 2 appeal), 1996.

By the year 2000, it will be impossible to get agreement, anywhere in the civilized world, that it is not OK to be lesbian or gay.

Advertisement in the homosexual newspaper
San Francisco Sentinel, 1993.

FIFTEEN

Sunrise comes first as a tint of pink and purple across the peaks. Then dawn descends in a curtain of vibrant gold, spreading down the slopes to the timberland below.

Lying on his stomach against an outflung granite boulder, John slips his infrared sensor back over his eyes for a look at the valley trail, far below him in the golden light. At this hour few people venture on the trail, but the ultrasensitive sensors often pick up the signatures of deer and elk on the move. Yesterday John even spotted a herd of bighorn sheep, switching quickly to binoculars to watch the graceful beasts clamber across a sheer rock face.

At the moment only a few deer appear on the glowing monitor.

Lying beside him, his scout tutor Tom sees it first — a lone backpacker emerging from a thick stand of ponderosa pines. He points and John looks over. Through the spotting scope he makes out a stocky, masculine frame, tiny in his sights. Short hair. Bulky pack.

John focuses and fights to steady his hands. Is it a woman? She obviously is not wearing the small infrared signal bracelet they have all been given to wear on their occasional hikes across the valley. The telltale quivering

129

glow is nowhere to be seen. Tom gives him a knowing nod. Trying to ignore the sudden pull of fear at the pit of his stomach, John turns on his headset and whispers. "Intruder alarm. Sentry Two."

Deep inside the mountain, Bruce leans back against a stack of mildewed army surplus boxes. He is trying his best not to look at Vern, who sits impassive at the table. He looks instead down to his feet and slowly shakes his head, as though his worn hiking boots present some deep and unsolvable dilemma.

"Vern, there's good news and bad news. The good news is, we have a place for you to go. Your transportation plan is all set."

"Great. And …"

"Bad news is, we can't tell you what the plan is."

"What?"

"We can't tell you anything more until you've made up your mind."

Vern closes his eyes for a long moment, trying to quell the rising flood of frustration. He blinks back open to the glare of the cavern's bare bulbs and clenches his fists. "Do you guys think I'm sitting around here flipping coins over whether I should go rescue my wife and daughter?"

He turns to them each in turn: Bruce, the muscular courier Dave, Myrna the middle-aged widow with an ocean of pain in her eyes. "I don't know how!" He sweeps his hands through his scalp and grasps strands of hair, pulling hard enough to feel it. "How do I break into my house through a police guard? How do I take back my daughter when her location is secret? I'm not James Bond."

Hearing his voice's pitch rising, he throws up his hands. "I've been wracking my brain. I stayed awake all night trying to figure it out."

"Maybe that's because you shouldn't go back at all," Myrna says.

"Vern, please. We know you're in an awful situation. No one's blaming you. But until you decide what you're going to do about your family, until they're all here and you're ready to leave, we can't tell you anything about your destination."

David leans forward across the table, his triceps bulging to hold him steady. "Don't you see it's for your own protection? You go down there and get caught, and eventually they'll find a way to get you to tell. They'll wear you down. They'll offer deals you can't refuse."

"Maybe I should take Frank up on his offer. Maybe he's right. Maybe you guys are too soft on this issue, and we oughta be waging war against these people."

"I'll tell you something about Frank," Bruce says, as he closes his eyes slowly and exhales. He opens them again and smiles faintly. "Vern, have you ever heard of the Walldensians?"

"No. Doesn't ring a bell."

"The Walldensians were a group of Christians in Italy and Switzerland during the Renaissance years, who disagreed with mixing of church and state. You might call them the first Protestants, only at first, they didn't try to split from the Catholic Church; they only wanted to reform it from within, to freely practice their faith. And of course, they were branded heretics."

Bruce sits down and crosses his legs, warming up to the story. "Don't worry, Vern. There's a reason why I'm telling you this. See, when they first started getting persecuted, the Walldensians were absolutely opposed to all forms of violence, so instead of retaliating they moved their villages farther and farther away from their oppressors, up into the mountains. And they got more creative; they even developed a network of these anonymous circuit priests to travel around between them. A typical, peaceful Christian response. But eventually, the firebrands among them started getting more vocal, and when the French attacked on Easter week of 1655, killing and raping thousands, the

Walldensians blew their stack. They organized a militia, and started using guerilla tactics. At first, they were successful. They won their freedom for, oh, a couple of months. Eventually, though, the local ruler broke all his promises, united with the French and tightened the noose. And within a few years, thousands of Walldensians had been killed, imprisoned, forced to recant their faith — they were all but wiped out. It was genocide."

"Bruce is quite a history buff," Myrna said to Vern with an apologetic smile.

"That's right, I am," he continued. "History matters. But my point is this. If you want to get killed for Jesus and make a big commotion doing it, then take Frank's road. With him, that's an almost guaranteed outcome. You'll become another tragic sidenote in the history books, and nothing more. But if you want to see your family again, if you want to make a difference in this world that God put you in, then I'd urge you to think twice before following the firebrands."

"I will. I just want you to know that I'm tired of sitting around here wondering how to bring my family back together."

"Vern," Bruce says plaintively, "I understand. And I promise you, no one will pressure you to leave the Refuge while you're still making up your mind. You stay here as long as you need. And if there's anything we can get for you, any kind of intelligence we might help with, you let us know."

Suddenly, the door creaks open and a frightened face peeks in. "Alarm, guys. You better get out here."

When Sonya reaches mid-valley, she notices a set of tracks leaving the trail and heading up into the brush, into the flank of Mount Huron. The prints are fresh, and the point of departure makes no sense. Just as she stops and begins to tell herself, better check this out, could be something … her breath will not return to normal, she cannot replenish her lungs, she pants harder and harder trying to gulp in more air, then in her panic she remembers her doctor warning her about pulmonary edema, the high altitude illness, and its increased risk for people with AIDS. Just as it dawns on her that yes, this is exactly what's happening here, her world spins furiously into a dark grey tunnel, and then instantly turns black.

Without a sound, she collapses into a stretch of high grass, her motionless body watched only by clumps of nodding columbine and Indian paintbrush.

Four men in black clothes, bundles of electronic apparatus upon their backs, emerge into the cool alpine morning. The night's clouds are lifting slowly, clinging to the peaks in vast, majestic shreds. Last night's hidden valley is today's route to the ramparts.

Steve reaches the cliff's edge first, reaches around him and produces a small tripod. He swiftly sets it upon the rock and shrugs off a small pack from which he pulls an oversized infrared scope. The other men sprawl beside him, also pulling out equipment — military nightvision goggles, radios, headsets. Finally, the last of them arrives. Frank reaches around and shoulders a hunting rifle.

After several long moments, Steve's whisper comes first. "Where is it?"

"I don't see anything."

"Me neither."

Bruce presses the radio and speaks into the small microphone held by a black wire to the edge of his mouth. "Base, were they sure they saw someone?" A metallic voice answers in his ear. "Absolutely. Lone backpacker. Wearing camo and a big pack." Bruce blows out a long breath. "Sounds pretty serious ..."

"Wait! I'm picking up a signature," says Vern. "It's — right off the trail. Two hundred yards off onto the approach."

"Oh no."

"Looks like the person's lying down. Can any of you guys see anything?"

"I do," answers a boyish voice, belonging to John. "It's a woman. There's something the matter with her. She's not resting; she's on her stomach, pack's on top of her."

Steve leans back, the dilemma twisting across his face. "Do you see any police gear on her? Gun? Radio?"

Tommy's voice: "Negative."

"Describe her."

"Stocky. Pink bandana. Short spiky hair. Big boots. Camo."

Frank turns to Vern. "Was your back clean when you came in here?"

"I have no idea."

So they wait. A long silence falls upon them. The sun travels across the sky, the wind blows without tiring, and the clouds trace their random courses over the valley. Finally, when they have nearly forgotten their reason for sitting up here, Steven sits up, a resolute expression upon his face.

"Tommy, any movement?"

"Negative."

"All right. I want you to execute your very best full-stealth reconnoiter."

Frank bristles immediately. "You sending the boy down there?"

"That's right. He's the best scout we've got."

"Are you crazy? That boy won't handle her if she's one of them …"

"Frank, we've practiced this a dozen times. Tommy is a natural. Besides, what if she's one of us? Another seeker looking for cover? You gonna let her die?" Bruce touches his earpiece to transmit again. "Tommy, if she speaks to you, total cover, okay? You're a backpacker. Your father is up at Lake Ann."

"Roger. Going down."

The boy tosses aside his headset, scrambles from the

rock perch and begins jogging downwards across the boulder field. Within seconds he has disappeared into the profusion of rocks.

Her blurred, careening world blinks back on again, for just a moment. It has been an eternity now since she has been able to breathe. Her chest is on fire. She can almost feel her lungs heaving inside her. Her head swims wildly, her eyes roll around like those of a baby.

She does not see the boy's eyes watch her from behind a nearby tree, then dart out of sight. Nor does she see them reappear a few seconds later, much closer this time. She has no idea a Scout is advancing on her with the silence and invisibility of an Apache tracker.

She blacks out again and after another eternity, opens up her eyes onto a face peering over her, male, young, eyebrows furrowed in concern. Like a phantom, the face recedes to the bottom of a quivering grey well at the center of her vision, then returns.

"Are you okay?" The voice is boyish, high-pitched.

She grunts in pain and frustration. She wants to answer, to give this kid a suitably sarcastic answer to his dim-witted question, but she can only wait until the top of a breath, then utter the words on the breath's way down. "No! I gotta — gotta get down — trailhead ..."

"Is anybody with you?"

"NO!!"

"Are you meeting anybody?"

She would like to think about that question, analyze it just a second, but her mind will not settle on any thought but a mindless craving for relief. "No!"

After a brief pause, the boy's hands grip her just below the armpit and her horizon starts to pitch sideways, then right itself. She is moving. He pulls her hands out and cinches her arms tight. Spruce trees begin to file slowly past her. This is good, she thinks, I'm going somewhere.

Two hundred yards away, hidden in the dim light of tree cover, four rifle barrels point straight ahead, moving slightly with the trio's slow progress. The woman may be sick, but then again, maybe she's not. She might be an awfully good actress. If she makes any sudden moves against her benefactor, she won't live to make another — Frank, for one, will make sure of that.

The boy and his burden disappear from sight. Four camouflaged figures dart from behind the trees and jog quietly to new positions.

Thankfully, she has only progressed a quarter-mile from the Wilderness Trailhead before her collapse. Still, Tommy reaches the gate exhausted, gasping for breath, stepping sideways to pull her through.

She has not stopped panting. "Over there," she huffs, pointing at her truck. As he pulls her the last few feet she removes one hand and reaches down into her pocket to fish for keys. As she yanks her pullover back, the dark shape of a gun holster peeks briefly out. Tommy's eyes go wide.

And Sonya, at once, has noted the reaction. They have descended a thousand feet and her lungs are improving a little; she feels stronger. She pulls out the keys and lurches against the truck's door, flails at the keyhole and finally connects. She flings the door open and then whirls around, falling back against the truck, holding forth one extended hand.

Tommy sees the gun in a flash of grim amazement, and only then does he see the inside of her cab: a shotgun lying in the floorboard, a radio mounted in the dash.

"All right, boy. Who are you? You a Scout, helping a poor lady out like that?"

He shifts nervously, looking around for help.

"ANSWER ME!"

Behind the trees, Frank cannot resist a soft, guttural curse. He looks over to Bruce behind an adjacent tree, his eyes afire. "I gotta take her out! I'm gonna do it!"

"No! We're not killing anybody!"

"She's got a gun on him!"

"She's not going to shoot that boy! Besides, what if you miss?" Bruce yanks the binoculars up to his face — the woman has now leaned inside the truck's cab to do something ... through the scope he sees a dark, round shape in her hand.

Then like a blast of wind the realization hits him. "She's calling in! The radio!"

Frank pulls his trigger and with a roar the windshield trembles into a jagged spiderweb; Tommy recoils and looks back at them, waving his hands below him. *No, hold your fire. Come down here* ... So all at once the men are sprinting down the slope, crazed, imprudent yells bellowing from their lungs. They reach Tommy who turns, shock engulfing his face. He shrugs and points at the woman.

The radio microphone dangles by its cord from the truck's door, under her open hand. Bruce edges forward muzzle first, nudges the door further open. She has simply passed out, her strength extinguished by the strain of the encounter. But a voice hisses from the radio. "Lavender five, we copy your position. Evac and standby for back-up. Over ..."

The trail unspools madly beneath their feet. No words now, only anxious intakes of breath and the pumping of hearts in their ears. They no longer see the mountains, the sun or the beauty all around them; their minds are aflame with panic and the fear of what's behind them, back there at the road which could begin, at any moment, to disgorge into this valley their worst nightmare.

They try to imagine their companions high above them, rushing through the evacuation plans, the dark tunnels ringing with shouts and anxious cries, rucksacks being stuffed with clothes and food and last remaining possessions, each one mentally preparing for another whirlwind of fear and pursuit and, worst of all, uncertainty.

The four men, Tommy and John reach the junction with the mountain trail and disperse into cover, half in the upslope trees, half in the willow brush lining the creek. After a minute, having verified the absence of pursuit, the downslope three rejoin Bruce and the others in the timber.

Bruce finally catches his breath, switches the headset on and speaks between gulps of breath. "Steve? Steve? Did you mayday?" Soon a reply crackles in his earpiece. "Good," Bruce replies. "Steve, there's no time for normal evac. She called in the position, so they could be at the gate right now. Here's what you do. Everyone up there goes to Madallen. Copy? You go there now. The others and I will cross the saddle into Taylor. We'll signal when we've got transport at Texas Creek. It may be awhile before things cool down enough. All right, you be careful ..."

After all the hours listening to procedures in the cramped situation room, Vern understands Bruce's breathless rambling perfectly. Another abandoned shaft, Madallen Mine, lies high atop the ridge only a mile and a half from their Huron site. It too is equipped with food and blankets, waiting dormant for an emergency such as this.

Their route will take them in the opposite direction, climbing fast towards the westward pass and over into the vast valley of Taylor Park. They set off at a brisk pace up the trail towards Lake Ann, crossing the creek on an improvised bridge, climbing through forest for a mile, then rejoining the creek in a shallow, climbing valley. Fleetingly, in that moment before fear and fatigue regain control, Vern remembers his father's tales about elk inhabiting such places.

Pausing briefly for rest beside a flooded meadow, he sets his hand on John's shoulder. "You're doing great, son," he says, smiling. He's never been so proud of the boy. Still fighting for air, John grins knowingly.

They climb steeply out of the valley and emerge at timberline, on a sloping plateau which culminates at the base of a towering chasm in the mirrored waters of Lake Ann. They rest lying stomach-down in deep, fragrant grasses, as Bruce silently scopes the valley below for activity. He lowers the binoculars and nods slowly in encouragement. Nothing yet. Just then a rumble comes upon them and —

a sudden burst of wind, the grass around them flying madly about them, a dark shadow lunging murderously overhead, blades slicing the sunlight, a staccato thunder chopping apart the sky in an ear-splitting cacaphony —

and in one second the shape of a Chinook helicopter hurtles past and takes shape below them, roaring away downslope. Bruce is yelling something unintelligible, but judging from his face pressed flat into the ground he is telling them to stay down. It is possible, Vern realizes, that despite the immediacy of its commotion above their heads, the chopper has failed to spot them.

Already a mile away, the helicopter banks sharply and buzzes the lower slopes of Mount Huron, entering a steep turn. They watch, hardly breathing, as it circles back to face them, but it does not advance. Hovering over the lower stretches of the valley, it lands slowly beside the distant trail.

Instantly, Bruce is on his feet. "Come on! Let's go!" He almost jogs now, skirting the shore, then leads them onto a small game trail which snakes upwards towards a low saddle in the surrounding peaks.

The sudden fear has now sapped all their remaining strength, and as the altitude increases, the hard work becomes agony. Crossing a grassy ledge before the final climb, Frank begins wheezing loudly. He clenches his teeth and grabs his side.

Bruce grabs his shoulder. "It's okay. We'll slow down the pace." Vern glances at John, then closes his eyes for the briefest of moments. "Lord, please help us make it. Just over the top. Please."

They start again, and soon Vern and John both begin feeling, instead of terminal exhaustion, the deep stirrings of a second wind. At once their legs seem unwilling to stop; instead, they feel fully capable of churning on forever. In this state of furious determination they reach the top, round the crest and emerge onto majesty — there, under a bracing blue sky, ringed by sprawling mountains, stretch the broad forests of Taylor Park four miles away.

"Over here!" Bruce yells into the harsh summit wind, scurrying towards the cover of a large boulder cluster. The six of them crouch and then, one by one, collapse on the rocky ground.

Bruce points down to the blue patch of Taylor Park Reservoir and the scattering of brown buildings at its eastern flank. "There! That's where the backup van is. A couple days from now, when we're ready to evacuate the Madallen, we'll rendezvous there." He turns to Vern and shouts. "Now the question is, Vern, are you coming with us? We're gonna disperse and take our routes. What are you gonna do?"

"You can't help me with this?"

"Not now, Vern! All bets are off now. We'll be lucky not to get caught! So what are you gonna do?"

Vern turns back into the wind, his mind fleeing gridlock. He tries to think, and finally forces his mind into action. The men watch him, eyes burning in the unrelenting wind.

"You gotta make up your mind, Vern. Make a decision — NOW!"

*... consensus grows among mental health profes-
sionals that homophobia, the irrational fear and
hatred of homosexuals, is a psychological abnormality that interferes with the judgement and reliability
of those afflicted.*

Dr. Richard Isay, Cornell Medical College psychiatrist, author of *Being Homosexual*, and chairman of
the American Psychiatric Association's Committee
on Gay, Lesbian and Bisexual issues.

SIXTEEN

She barely hears the knock upon the door. The couch surrounds her as it has for days now, its soft cushions seemingly unwilling to let her rise.

Come on, Gail. Get going. Someone's here to visit.

She stands shakily, hoping it isn't the policeman again, the one who stands watch outside her door, asking in that quiet voice for another glass of water or a visit to the bathroom.

She opens the door and it's a woman standing there, about twenty, pretty, dressed in blue jeans and clunky black boots and a white button-down shirt. A legal pad hugged to her chest. "Mrs. Yates? I'm Cari Miner, from the *Boulder Daily Telegraph.*"

Oh! How could I have forgotten? "That's right. Come in, I just woke up from a nap." They walk into the living room and Gail's hand strays nervously to the blanket, picks it up from the sofa and folds it absent mindedly.

"Mrs. Yates, would you like me to come back another time? I can, you know."

"Call me Gail. No. That's all right. It's just — been a long day."

Her solicitude quickly dispensed with, the young woman

143

sits down in the love seat and begins earnestly toying with her pen, paper and tape recorder.

Gail does not know whether to sit or stand, or play hostess. "Would you like a glass of water or something?"

The reporter looks up at her quizzically, as if deciding whether accepting a drink will place too great a burden on her hostess. "No, thank you," she answers finally with a wan smile. "I'd rather just get started, if you don't mind."

"No." Gail sits where minutes ago she slept. As she sinks in, the weariness returns.

Cari suddenly seems charged with intense concern, her eyes flashing as she gazes compassionately at her subject. "I just can't imagine what it would be like to have your family ripped apart like this. Can you describe for our readers what that would feel like?"

Gail takes a deep breath, but no brilliant thought alights upon her. "Not really, actually. It's beyond words. How do I take something like what's happened and squeeze it down into a few sentences?"

"I understand." Cari's head shakes at those words, the pathos of Gail Yates weighing her features with sudden sorrow. She leans forward, as far towards her as the chair will allow. "Gail, all I want to do is tell your story. Will you help me do that?"

Gail takes a deep breath. "Yes. I will."

Sharply, Cari looks down again to her legal pad. "Tell me this. Do you think you've ever done anything wrong in your rearing of Heather?"

"*Ever?* Have I *ever* done anything wrong? Well, sure I have. Every parent makes mistakes. I once fed her stale peas that made her sick. I forgot to give her medicine one night when she had the mumps."

"Not that," Cari interrupts. "The beliefs. The homophobia."

"What — do you really think my husband told a four-year-old child the facts of life about *homosexuality?*" Gail almost feels better, letting her voice rise a little. "All we did is teach her that a family is a mommy and daddy. And mommies and daddies are girls and boys all grown up. That's it." The crushing sense of injustice descends on her, fresh again. "For that, I'm a child abuser?"

"But what if Heather's gay herself? What kind of signals does that send her about her own self-worth?"

Despite herself, Gail allows a bitter chuckle to escape. She looks down, shaking her head. What do you say to such a question? "Cari," she says slowly, still facing the floor, "anyone who believes people are born gay is entitled to their opinion. But they're not entitled to shove it down my throat. Or the throat of my family. We have the right to disagree, you know."

"So you don't see any hatred in your family's beliefs."

"No!" She's shouting now, she knows it. She feels better than she has in days. "The irony, the awful, unbelievable irony here, is that I've been declared a criminal and an insane person for teaching my kids basic Christian beliefs, had my child yanked away by the government, my husband and son are being hounded like dogs by the police, and I'm the one answering questions about why I'M HATEFUL!?!"

"Please, Gail. I understand. I'm here to help. I'm here to bring your story to the people of this city."

Her anger spent, Gail now feels tears pressing for release. "You just don't know." She runs her fingers through her hair, closes her eyes for a few seconds' respite. "You know, if you'd asked me four years ago, I might have told you I agreed with gay rights. It's the words in the label — 'gay' and 'rights.' I might have not agreed with the lifestyles, but sure, I would have said, gays have rights like everyone else."

She stands now. The momentum of her unburdening has animated her limbs. The tears fall freely, now. She lets them. "What I didn't know was how much hate and intolerance and hypocrisy there was in that movement. I don't like to think ill of other people, I really don't, so I didn't believe the signs. I didn't believe someone could preach about tolerance and diversity and lie so badly — the whole time working night and day to take away your most basic rights — speech, worship, belief, association — just because you disagree with them. How, how can anybody imagine that kind of cunning? Who would believe it? Unless it happened to you? Unless it's the story of your own life? I mean, how many times have I seen, in the paper, on the news, some noble activist talking about fairness and loving each other, and I remember his face because he's punched a dent in our car, or screamed obscenities in my children's faces?"

Minutes pass. Tears flow, and words. Soon she is racked by sobs — it seems she has saved until now all her tears of grief, not only for her family, but for the sense of justice she once knew, her pride in America, her conviction that good would always win. She wishes she could stop, and eventually, she does. If only this had not happened in front of a reporter. She covers her face in grief and embarrassment, and concentrates on breathing for a moment.

The young woman's eyes stare wide at her. She seems transfixed. "I think I understand. One last question. How do you think this is all going to turn out?"

Gail thinks a second, as if she's deciding right this second, for sure. "I don't know. I really don't. But I have this feeling God's not going to let us down."

"Wow." Cari stops writing, clicks off the cassette recorder on her knee. "Gail, that's gonna be more than enough for me. Thank you. Thank you so much for sharing with me what you're going through."

Gail smiles for the first time in the conversation. "You're welcome. Of course, you know I don't have high expectations from the *Boulder Daily Telegraph*."

"Don't worry," Cari says, swinging her pursestrap over her shoulder. "They're really not in the censorship business. I'm going to write the truth about what I've seen here today. You can count on that."

Gail stands by the open door, watching her leave.

"I will. Bye ． "

The next morning the policeman knocks once and opens the door, the newspaper in his hand. "Just thought you might want your *Telegraph* this morning."

Gail walks in from the kitchen, holds her hand out eagerly. "Yes, officer. I do."

He steps forward, smiling nervously at her. "Have you got a minute, Mrs. Yates?"

"Sure ..."

"You don't remember me, do you."

"No ..."

"I used to go to Second Baptist. You know, back when it was a ... you know. My wife and I attended for about a year or so. We moved out of town a ways, and it got to be so far to drive."

Her mouth will not function; she has absolutely nothing to say. For weeks she has regarded this man as the arm of government authority, and though she had noticed his extreme courtesy and kindness, she had never dreamed of this sort of link with the man.

"Well," he stammers, embarrassed by the awkward pause, "I just wanted to tell you in case you hadn't recognized me. I'm just doing my job, you know. I'm a law enforcement officer, so I have to enforce the law the citizens pass. It's not my choice. It's not something I'm happy about ..."

"I understand," Gail says. It gives her a feeling of power, being able to end the man's misery. "I do. I just wish these laws had never been passed in the first place."

"Me too. Well, I'll leave you to your paper. Good day."

The high price of hatred

Cari Miner
Boulder Daily Telegraph

Every day now, from the depths of her deep depression, Gail Yates waits on her couch, hoping every step on the sidewalk outside her door signals the return of her four-year old daughter, Heather.

But Heather Yates is not coming home. Boulder County Child Protection authorities have terminated Gail's parental rights for reasons which, while incomprehensible to her, remain quite serious in the eyes of the law. In fact, little Heather has already been outplaced from the New School into the care of an awaiting foster family somewhere in Colorado.

Authorities say Gail Yates has already injured her young daughter's emotional development with what they allege is the willful infliction of a form of abuse called parental homophobia. The terminology may be new, and it certainly remains a source of controversy to Colorado's members of the Radical Right, but psychological experts insist it denotes a serious social problem and health hazard across the country.

"What is homophobia?" Gail asks plaintively, tears rolling down her lined, troubled face. "Is it a real phobia, where somebody suffers from an irrational fear? Or is it just a difference of opinion? Because it seems to me this word is being used against anyone who happens to disagree with even a single item of the gay political agenda."

Mental health professionals disagree — which is why last year, they voted to add homophobia to their governing body's list of mental disorders. Richard Gibson, the renowned psychiatrist and chairperson of the American Therapy Association's Gay, Lesbian and Bisexual Caucus, states that "... all reputable mental health professionals agree that homophobia is a severe psychological abnormality which should be dealt with like any other pathology."

Such opinions, along with most issues of concern to cutting-edge educational disciplines, matter little to Gail. Locked in the iron grip of depression, she does not understand these things. She only knows the crushing weight of Heather's absence, along with that of her husband, Vern, who fled two months ago with their son John. Vern is currently sought on child abuse charges.

"This woman may not consider her beliefs hateful," explains an anonymous Boulder County child protection official, "but the fact is, they're not only hateful, but extremely damaging. No child should be consistently exposed to bigotry, whether it's expressed against racial minorities, the differently abled, or diverse sexual orientations."

Perhaps the most obvious sign of Gail Yates' emotional impairment is her own inability to accept the facts. Her imagination is filled with myriad conspiracy theories, where evil gay-rights activists and nefarious government agencies plot against her. She insists that God will find a way to reunite her family — pluck Heather from the child welfare system, then bring her fugitive husband and son back in the bargain.

Perhaps, like so many others who share her beliefs, she has grown a bit too reliant on miracles. As it will take a true miracle to budge Gail Yates from her staunch homophobia, it will take another still to restore the family shattered by her harmful beliefs.

"City desk, this is Cari."

"Cari, this is Gail. Gail Yates. Do you have a moment?"

"Sure. How can I help you?"

"I'll keep it short, Cari. I just wanted you to know how disappointed I was in your article. It's not so much that you were biased against me. I was prepared for that. But on a personal level, you betrayed me. You led me to believe you were starting to understand how I felt. You expressed sympathy. You used that sympathy to draw me out, to get me to talk. And you used what I said to attack me."

"I'm sorry. I didn't mean for the story to come out that way. Gail, I barely wrote any of that story. My editor really put the slant on it. That wasn't me."

"But you told me the paper wasn't into censorship. You said what you wrote stayed."

"I know. In this case, I guess I was mistaken. I'm very sorry."

"If that's true, then why don't spend a little time investigating the truth? I challenge you — go down to the Boulder Queer Collective and spend a few hours talking to them about what they stand for. And when you're through, if you still think I'm a hatemonger and they stand for tolerance, I want you to come here and tell me that to my face."

"Okay, you're on."

"Cari, you were in my home. You've looked into my eyes. Do you really think I'm filled with hate?"

Gail waits, listening. After awhile she wonders if the reporter has hung up. Then the answer comes, in a voice small and almost sad.

"No, I don't ..."

The offices of Boulder's Queer Collective remind Cari of all those movies about the radicals of the sixties, huddled in dingy Berkeley cubbyholes brimming with righteous anger, walls lined with posters proclaiming revolt, liberation and the coming Revolution. The grungy warehouse loft before her now radiates the same vibe — a sort of smoldering, low-level hum, an odd intensity that radiates from the level gazes of the lesbian volunteers and the angry graphics plastering the brick wall. But the posters before Cari today bear headlines the Vietnam protesters would never recognize. *Silence = death. Hate is not a family value. Homophobia kills. Witches heal. Celebrate diverse sexuality. Thank you for not breeding.*

The director, a dark-haired man in his early twenties, walks back to their table with two steaming mugs of coffee. He sets them down and slouches into a chair, cocking his blue-jeaned leg up over the arm and fixing her with a deep, handsome grin. "So, you're doing a background story on the Collective."

"Absolutely. I want to know what makes you tick."

He laughs soundlessly and looks down into his coffee. "I'll tell you what makes us tick. Tolerance. Compassion. Diversity."

"Tell me, is it possible for someone to oppose your goals

without being motivated by hate?"

"Not really. I know that sounds a little dogmatic, but you have to think about it. If you're standing up for tolerance, anyone who stands against you is, by definition, acting out of intolerance. When you're anti-hate, then those who oppose you are pro-hate. Bottom line."

"But what if they don't see it that way? What if they consider your goals excessive, or frightening?"

"Well, maybe it's possible for someone to disagree with us out of plain old ignorance. That's why we're working so hard to enlighten people about the importance of diversity. Once we educate America, we won't have any more problems with the kind of bigotry that has dominated this culture for so long."

"Paint me a picture, if you would. A picture of the kind of America you're working to bring about."

He leans back, tilting the chair backwards, smiling at the ceiling. "We're going to create an America where no one, no one at all, believes there's a single thing wrong with homosexuality. Where everyone understands how flexible sexuality really is. That, instead of some fixed point on a compass, it's a fluid line where anyone can find themselves at a different place at any given time." He stands and puts down the coffee, grasps the back of the chair. "In our America no one will ever feel uncomfortable or looked-down on or disapproved of because of their sexual identity. That's the essence of queer theory, you know. Labels are oppressive. The fact is, we're all stuck on this shifting scale of sexuality whether we like it or not. No one is gay or straight or any one thing. We're all queer. Someday that'll be as universally accepted as the curvature of the earth."

"Is there any room in this America for people who disagree with you?"

"What, you mean the religious right and all that ..."

"No, not just them. Anybody — anyone who doesn't share your views. Where do they fit in?"

He lets out a loud guffaw. "Honestly? They don't. I mean,

let's face it. Their beliefs are wrong. Hateful. Destructive. Why should we make room for that in America?"

"Well, you talk about diversity and pluralism. Surely that doesn't mean much, if you're only advocating diversity for those who see things your way."

He looks down, his head nodding in preoccupation, then looks up suddenly. "You're right. Diversity and pluralism make great campaign slogans. But in the strict sense of the word, that's not what we're after. Why make room for beliefs that divide people, that make people feel oppressed and alienated, views that spread hatred?"

"One could argue that it's the controversy itself that's dividing people. Not necessarily the views of any one side."

He looks at her crossly. "Listen. I can appreciate your playing the devil's advocate, here. But knock it off. You're starting to sound like some kind of right-wing agitator."

"Me? I'm asking questions. I'm just getting you to explain your logic."

"Isn't that what I've been doing?"

"Not completely. I'm just trying to clarify."

He jams his hands in his jean pockets, his eyes avoiding her. "Have you got the background you wanted?"

She looks up from her notepad, giving him a sullen glare. "I guess so."

"Good. By the way, is your editor a part of this ... fact-finding mission?"

"My editor? No. Reporters usually locate sources on their own. Why do you ask?"

"Nothing. I'm just not used to this kind of treatment from the *Telegraph.*"

She feels her body freeze. Something about the way he said that, some tiny gleam of grievance in his eyes, has set all of her alarms ringing at once. "What kind of treatment is that, may I ask?"

He looks away from her. Glaring past her, he almost seems angry at something in the sky, beyond the windows. "No comment, Ms. Miner. Goodbye ..."

A single bulb burns over the archive room's midnight silence. Heavy-lidded with fatigue, Cari watches a blur of black and white stream past the screen of the microfiche reader.

She may be weary, but her every instinct screams to her that the activist's parting comment had betrayed some smelly little secret, a stench emanating from somewhere far too close to home. Why did the man expect to be handled with kid gloves? What kind of favorable treatment has her paper given these people, anyway? She's been a reporter long enough to know that she will not sleep until she digs it up.

She turns away from the microfiche reader, drops a bulging story folder marked "Queer Collective" into her lap, and begins rifling through the thick stack of notes. Almost midway through, she holds up a small note sheet and squints to discern its scribbled handwriting.

Then she feels her blood run cold.

Of course. The Dewayne Page suicide.

She had been a cub reporter when the story broke. After a week's worth of grim headlines about a homophobic triumph in the legislature — which was, ironically, to be their last — the tragedy had given gay rights forces a much-needed jolt of moral outrage, a chance to retake the high ground through soundbites brimming with righteous indignation and eloquent grief.

And the paper had milked it for all it was worth. Cari remembers the senior reporters muttering angry condemnations of fundamentalist Christians over their word processors as they slammed the story home.

"Anti-gay victory causes man's suicide."

"Homophobia steals man's will to live."

Dewayne Page, a gay man suffering from the latter stages of AIDS, had not only taken an overdose of sleeping pills after the homophobes' victory, but he had left a suicide note blaming the hatred and bigotry of his fellow

Coloradans. "I don't care to live in the fresh hell these hatemongers have prepared for me ..."

The headlines had lingered for nearly a week. The story had galvanized gay activists, who began carrying a black coffin in their protests and chanting that homophobia had taken its first victim. For a month afterwards, the item had occupied a line in nearly every media account of the gay rights issue. "The poisoned atmosphere in Colorado even led one gay man to commit suicide rather than face the raging homophobia in our state ..."

The gay militants had been given their martyr. And then, unexpectedly, the story had disappeared overnight.

Even then, fresh in the business, Cari had known that a juicy item like this one wouldn't evaporate of its own free will. She remembers puzzling over its absence, then asking a few veterans who had mumbled evasive replies and turned away.

Now she knows why ...

The scrap of paper bears four scribbled lines. "Second suicide note? Police not talking. Possible investigation — call Collective."

This time he does not even bother to greet her, or even sit down for the conversation. He stands in the entryway, hands dug deep in his pockets, with an expression vacillating between a frosty smile and outright hostility.

"This will just take a minute," she says, readying her pen. Normally she would relish every second of this. This is the moment every reporter dreams of — to speak the damning question, to watch it find its mark upon the slackening, blood-draining face of a guilty man hearing the bells of his personal doom. Right now, however, that joy is absent. She cannot forget that her employer is the guilty party every bit as much as the man before her. Nevertheless, she must know.

"I want to ask you a follow-up question. About Dewayne Page."

His eyes turn cold. The sight of it chills her; the humanity draining out, leaving her under the glare of two vacant sockets. He speaks slowly. "Yes. A sad story."

"Very sad. I wanted to ask you about a police investigation into suspicions that you and other Collective leaders goaded Page into killing himself and writing that note."

He looks away, his breath exhaling slowly. It seems to Cari, watching the firestorm cycle through his eyes, that he's deciding whether to act shocked at the implication, feign weary familiarity, or just furiously cut her off. Finally he looks back her way, but his eyes only meet hers for a second. His voice is low and even. "You're not about to resurrect that old fairytale, are you ..."

"I'm not aware that the story was ever alive to begin with. Seems the police found a second suicide note telling his parents that he'd killed himself for a good cause. Saying that you and two other Collective leaders had been over the night before to ask him for the supreme sacrifice. The story was never run and the police investigation just kind of fizzled out."

He turns on her, a different person now; his voice and eyes crackling with an energy like an inner fire. "That's because Dewayne Page was a very despondent young man in the last stages of AIDS. He had attempted suicide twice before. The homophobic victory was all it took."

"So you're denying the allegation?"

His chin jerks sideways in an involuntary twitch. A frosty candor enters his voice. "Why are you doing this? I thought we and the paper had an understanding."

Her heart sinks. A brief rush of nausea overtakes her. This is what she feared, a scenario briefly considered and quickly banished to the outer reaches of her imagination. "You mean — an understanding to kill the story? I must have missed that meeting ..."

Suddenly his confidence is back. With a jolting motion towards her which she almost mistakes for aggression, he thrusts his outstretched hand towards her. "Why don't you

call your editor next time? Have a good day, Ms. Miner."
She does not return the handshake.

Her editor's summons is already upon her desk when she returns. A hastily scribbled note. *See me. Now.* She walks in and closes the door behind her without being asked. He swivels around from his computer, seemingly unsurprised that she is the intruder. He speaks with hardly a second's pause, his voice trembling with anger. "What were you thinking? I've got their whole board of trustees, along with the whole gay and lesbian leadership of Boulder climbing my case. Screaming that we're out on some kind of a witch hunt. Do you know how powerful these people are? How badly they can hurt this paper?"

"I sure do."

"So what in the world were you doing?"

She stares at the floor, knowing how idiotic this will sound. "It was a challenge. Gail Yates dared me to dig up the truth about the Queer Collective. And I found something."

His fifty-year-old jowls blossom into the red mottled pattern every reporter has come to dread. "You went and incited the gay community because some homophobic woman *dared* you?"

"That's right. And I don't like what I found. Larry, did the paper agree to bury the truth about Dewayne Page because it would have embarrassed the gay community? Did you do that? Because I'm not sure I can live with that."

He clasps his hands behind his head. His anger seems passed. He runs the edge of his fingernails briskly over the edge of his desk calendar, now the paternal teacher.

"Cari, you went to a progressive journalism school, so I know you know this. Neutrality and impartiality in journalism is dead, it's a thing of the past; a sick, dead past. We're not here to inform. Information is raw data, and we're more than glorified typists, blindly repeating the where, what, why and how. Today we go further. We enlighten.

We move people. We raise the consciousness."

"So ..."

"So," he interrupts, "you owe nobody the least explanation about objectivity or lack of bias. When it's so clear who's wrong and who's right on an issue, forget objectivity. Be biased, and be proud of it."

She stands to leave. She feels strangely grieved by the lecture, although he was right — this is how she was taught in journalism school. "The thing is, Larry, I've looked in that woman's eyes, and I'm starting to wonder. Between her and the Collective, it's becoming a lot less clear who the hatemongers are."

His words are cold and level. "You're off the story, Cari. If I find you doing any work on the Yates family, or anything related to gay rights, I'll fire you."

Dear Gail,

I wanted you to know that I took your suggestion. I visited your opponents. I took the pulse of the gay rights movement, if you will. I guess what I found is no surprise to you, but it's sure rocked my world.

I remember that you challenged me to come visit you, look you in the eye and say that you were the hateful one. Well, I can't come see you. I'm in big trouble with the paper because of your challenge, and I can't be seen going to your house. But I can write and tell you this: they have a lot less tolerance for your point of view than you seem to have for theirs. And they sure have a lot less integrity.

I don't know what to make of this. I am, in the main, wholeheartedly committed to progressive issues, which include the environment, reproductive freedom and gay rights. I'm very confused right now.

No matter what, I'm sorrier than ever for the way my paper treated you. And I really do feel sorry for your situation. I wish you the best.

Cari Miner

1984. *The Seattle City Council considers an ordinance making it a crime to "discredit, demoralize, or belittle another person by words or conduct" based on sexual orientation.*

1994. *The government of Ontario, Canada, imposes a speech code law on its universities, banning comments about sexual orientation found to cause a "negative environment or climate." Students can file complaints if course work "hurt their feelings" or made them "uncomfortable." Speech overheard off-campus, at social functions, during academic work, even over the telephone, can be punished. Guilty students could be forced to apologize, suspended, ordered into "sensitivity training," even expelled.*

1995. *A federal district court affirms a New Jersey "gay rights" amendment which makes it illegal to say or print anything which could indirectly "promote discrimination" against homosexuals.*

SEVENTEEN

Vern would remember it later as a resolute decision, made in a time of crisis. But during the moment itself, standing atop the Continental Divide with the wind ripping through his hair, the assurance of what he would do had simply overtaken him.

He would return. He would defy every instinct of self-preservation and veer eastward, back toward Boulder. "I gotta go back," he had heard his voice mutter. "I gotta get my family back together if I die trying."

Without conscious intention his hand had found its way into Bruce's grip, a long and heartfelt handshake, and then gripped Johnny's shoulder as the two made their good-byes and thank-you's to the others.

Father and son had stood, their wooden legs resisting movement. Finally, feeling a resurgence of his will, Vern had forced his feet into motion, stepping forlornly downhill. They had turned back and waved, when suddenly Frank, his eyes once again filled with tears, had stepped out. "Wait! Tommy, will you go on to Refuge Two with the others and wait for me? This fool here's gonna need some help!"

They descend the southern slope of the Apostles, the yawning expanse of Taylor Park always before them. It is dangerous going — trying to minimize their exposure above treeline, they move down in long, almost running strides, their feet sliding through thick granite chunks with every step. Johnny, to his father's surprise, adapts to this gait best of all; he glides downward, hands outstretched, and soon moves far beyond the elder two.

Then, suddenly, he stops. Frantically speeding to catch up, Vern tries to catch a look at the sky. No sound but the wind; no choppers. When he reaches the boy, however, Johnny is smiling, holding a finger aloft. Frank and Vern follow his gaze to a ragged ridgeline, three hundred yards to their left. And there facing them stands a shocking patch of pure white — a mountain goat perched nonchalantly above a hundred-foot precipice. As their gaze sharpens they notice more: several females and their young grazing in a green patch far behind.

Vern smiles, sensing the intelligence and fierce curiosity in the animal's stare. Then, all at once, the goat is in motion, moving upwards with quick, heaving thrusts of his massive haunches. The sheer elevations they sweated to climb an hour ago now fall easily under the beast's effortless clamber. In twenty seconds he is a speck on the ramparts high above them.

"Let's go," Frank finally rumbles. "We gotta get off this rock."

They make camp that night along the banks of Texas Creek, a stream flowing west from the high basins they have just left. They have no food, but Frank finds a few matches in a pants pocket, and soon a campfire warms them. "I was a Scout myself," he tells them, "back when it was legal."

As father and son warm themselves eagerly, Frank walks away without a word, into the forest. A minute later they hear him rooting around in the trees behind them. Soon he returns, carrying three large, dusty rocks. With an old man's weary moan, he walks forward, steps right up to the flames, and drops the stones into the fire.

He turns around with a mysterious grin, never offering them a second's explanation. Next he shows them how to stuff leaves, moss and pine needles between their coats and shirts. The solution is far from comfortable, but soon they feel the night chill retreating from their bodies. Then, groaning good-heartedly with each bend forward, Frank leads them in building a debris hut large enough for the three of them to sleep in, piled high with everything they scrape from the forest floor. In the center of its floor, he digs into the dirt and makes a small hole. In an hour they are finished. The structure is crude but functional, and what's more, the exercise has kept the cold further at bay.

Johnny eagerly crouches to enter, but Frank warns him off. He has one last trick up his sleeve.

Walking over to the dwindling fire, he uses two long, green sticks to pick up the now red-hot rocks. He walks carefully, carries them over to the shelter and buries them inside.

"Now, we're ready to sleep," he says proudly.

And they do, amazed at the warmth Frank's shelter and his improvised heater can generate. They wake up hungry but rested. Within two hours of leaving camp they have hiked down through the pine forests and elk meadows to the collection of cabins and convenience stores marking the sum total of human civilization in Taylor Park. Frank ventures in to call a friend from the pay phone. Late that afternoon, as they wait beside a nearby road to Cotton-wood Pass, a friend's Jeep Cherokee swerves aside, its front passenger door flung open.

They drive eastward along the darkened lanes of Inter-state 70. As he moves closer to the Denver area, and the mountain towns pass by — Frisco, Georgetown, Idaho

Springs — Vern feels a growing sense of dread, as if he is pushing through concentric circles of evil. Some sinister, invisible resistance seems to part reluctantly before him.

Their companions do not help the mood; their conversation consists of endless condemnations and pessimistic ramblings about the state of the country. "Look at that," says their driver, a rough young man in his early thirties, as they pass a highway interchange. "You see those lights up there? Government's got video cameras, and radios, so they can monitor everybody who goes by."

"I'm telling you, Auschwitz was nothing," Frank says, "compared to what the New World Order has in store for us."

Johnny looks over, alarmed. "Really?" he asks his father. Vern turns his face to the boy. "Don't worry, son. If that happens, Christ will get us through it. It's all right."

Finally, late that night, they cross the hump of Genesee Pass on the interstate and the jeweled constellations of Denver tilt forward into their view.

"So," Frank asks, turning to him. "You got a plan?"

Vern has been silent for a half hour now, thinking of just that. "I think I do for Heather. What worries me is Gail. She's got police watching her. We may have to just stake out the house and wait."

Frank nods slowly, watching the city lights. "What's your plan for Heather?"

"Have you got a computer?" Vern asks their driver.

"No, but my brother does. He lives two miles away."

"Does he have a modem?"

It feels good, sitting in front of a keyboard, after all this time. He has forgotten he was once good at this. Within minutes his fingers remember their mastery of the keys; the old codes and languages start seeping back into his conscious mind. It feels good, too, knowing the reason for returning to the computer like this. He feels alert, his head rings with the prowling energy of the hunter.

His company once held a contract to modify the State of Colorado databases, so he has a working knowledge of their software architecture. Frank brings him coffee. Johnny sleeps behind him. He remains there all night, a roomful of sleeping fugitives lit only by the glow of cathode rays.

Frank awakens with the first light of dawn, and quietly steps over to the work area. "You found anything?"

Vern turns back with a look halfway between preoccupation and triumph. He says nothing, but the steel in his glance persuades Frank to look at the screen. The data entry screen is filled with boxes and brightly colored fields. But there, bigger than life, glows a name.

```
Yates, Heather    FOSTER HOME   184 Fairbrook Lane Denver
```

They drop Johnny off at a park one mile away and drive off.

He feels strange, all of a sudden walking around like a normal kid on a normal afternoon. All around him families are playing softball and touch football. He smells burgers and baby's diapers being changed.

It all feels so alien now. Especially since his father, who just dropped him off, might never come back. He tries not to think about it too much. After a few moments quietly watching the scene, he walks over, sits down against a tree trunk, and anxiously waits.

She is so glad to be out of the hospital, out doing her job once again. Stakeout. Denver has countless streets like this one, shaded by old sycamores and lined with restored

Victorian homes. But Sonya doesn't own one. When Liberation Day comes, she has promised herself she'll take one all for her own. Redistribution of wealth: kick the rich out and see how they like it applying for public housing, or hunting for apartments to make some landlord rich.

After the secret camp's discovery and the dispersal of its occupants, she has replayed the contingencies a hundred times — lying in the hospital, during the van ride back to Denver, in the hours waiting for her strength to return. There's one mystery she cannot process. Why did that boy risk his freedom to help her, to save her life? How could someone infected with that kind of hate and bigotry do something that seemed so selfless? Maybe he's too young to be a real homophobe yet. She wants to settle for that answer, but somehow it rings hollow in her mind. Better still to forget the question and concentrate on Vern Yates.

She knows he'll come; she can feel it.

He's got to. No self-righteous Christian male ever leaves his adoring harem behind that easy. He's gonna show. He's gonna make a play, and I'm gonna nail his lily-white, heterosexual hide. I'll make the papers, and a month from now I'll be kicking back in a state investigator's job, drawing health insurance. No more freelance fieldwork. No more cringing in public health clinics, feeling like a beggar for wanting to live.

Two o'clock. Ten minutes later, Irene Goldfarb drives up as usual, the shiny black Suburban with the small blond head of Heather Yates barely protruding above the passenger window. The unsuspecting Mrs. Goldfarb turns alongside the house and the car disappears beyond its northern side, lost to Sonya's gaze inside the sheltering walls of her white-collar, domestic cocoon.

You're not so safe, honey. If I weren't here, you'd be nothing but fundamentalist bait. Irene has only been told of increased security, possible surveillance. They have not met. It's better that way; a goody-goody like her would be out here with cookies and lemonade, Sonya thinks with a laugh. She guesses they serve a purpose, these guilty-rich liberals rationalizing their capitalistic success with trembling, cringing forays into the inner city and obsequious homages to the oppressed classes. Trying to kiss up to the rage they themselves have created, a rage which will someday destroy them too.

Sonya has tried to understand why they support her cause so fervently, these comfortable professionals positively bubbling over with pious declarations of compassion and diversity. What do they know of alienation, of injustice?

So many times, she has watched the leaders of the Gay Revolution shield these essential allies from the full details of their plans. "Informational discretion," they call it. She just knows that if the liberal elite ever caught wind of how aggressively she and her comrades plan to smash all Judeo-Christian oppression and throw open the doors of sexual freedom and diverse orientations, they'd drop their support in a heartbeat.

Oh, well. Their day will come.

She looks down to the cola between her knees and suddenly a commotion flashes by her open window; the dark protrusion of a shotgun barrel materializes against her forehead, held in a steady hand. A white guy in his late fifties, grey hair. "Hands on that dash, honey," says a gravelly voice.

As soon as she palms the dashboard, the bitter weight of her failure sinking fast into her guts, the other door opens and another man lurches in beside her. He doesn't pause; his hand immediately reaches down to her radio and pulls back a fistful of connecting wires. He looks at her, a fast-weaving Caucasian face, lost to furious movement.

"Hi. I'm here for my family."

It all happens fast, her door opens and the older man slides in too, pushing her to the center of the seat. "We're not going to hurt you," the younger one says, breathing hard from exertion. "You and my friend here're gonna go back to our truck and have a nice little sit while I," he snaps her holster from her belt and picks up her deputy's badge from the seat, "have some quality time with my daughter. Which is a crime, isn't it?"

She doesn't answer. As Frank handcuffs her wrists behind her and, looking around carefully, pulls her from the vehicle, she gives herself over to the rage, lets the blackness drift over her mind. This is it. If she can kill either one of these men, she will. And she'll love it.

He moves along the sidewalk as if he belongs to the neighborhood. He turns into the drive and walks to the door, knocks. The questioning face of Irene Goldfarb appears through the screen, scrutinizes the holster, the outstretched hand with the badge.

"Hello, Ma'am. I believe you've been told I was coming."

"Oh ... well, I heard there were going to be more patrols... "

"May I come inside? We need to go over a few precautions."

With a smile, she lets him inside. It seems so perverse to him that it takes this little piece of gold plate, rather than the reality of being Heather's father, to be granted admittance. They walk through paneled corridors to a family room and there she is, sitting at an oak table, crayon in hand, as she did so many times in their house. Vern's heart suddenly feels like it is going to rise through the top of his head and explode ...

"Honey," Irene begins, the girl still engrossed in her coloring book ...

"Honey," Vern now calls out, in the father's voice he has never forgotten, competing with this impostor parent. Those eyes from his tortured dreams rise at the sound of his voice — his voice alone, he notices — and the girlish face comes alive with a squeal of delight.

"Daddy!!"

It all happens in a flurry now — Heather's arms go up in a daughter's reflex and his hands pluck her swiftly from the chair, holding her tightly, just as he turns square to the woman who is drowning out Heather's squeals with piercing shrieks. He would say something, tell her he means her no harm, but his plan is to disregard her. He rushes by and runs for the front door.

The side door slaps. From the sidewalk two hundred yards back, Frank sees the two emerge from the house. Time to go. Vern has what he came for. Frank pulls the gearshift back and prepares to gun it. Curbside getaway, good and quick; that's the key.

"Just hang on," he mutters to Sonya beside him. "We'll drop you off safe and sound, a few miles from here, and we'll be on our way."

Handcuffed beside him, Sonya snarls and makes her move — in a grunting sideways lunge, she headbutts him solid in the forehead and, with a vicious punch of her left leg, stomps on his accelerator foot with all her might. She throws her torso on the steering wheel, writhing on top of the dazed Frank, and uses her outstretched elbow to crudely steer them towards the house. The street lurches past with the engine's growl then with a jarring bump the sidewalk too, and they're hurtling fast now, the lawn flashing by in a split second and she still has control of the steering wheel beneath her, twisting it against her body. They're not getting away in her vehicle. Not if it kills her. The house rushes up to meet them ...

On the porch, Vern scoops up his daughter and with a flying leap, clears the truck's oncoming path.

The squealing of tires and racing of engine abruptly end with a sickening metallic crunch — the truck smashes headfirst into the house, crumples the first few feet of wall and lurches to a sudden stop, half inside and half outside of what used to be the living room.

Locked inside the twisted metal, Frank senses throughout his body the distant ache of unfelt pain. He looks beside him and his eyes recoil at the sight of Sonya's blood-soaked head laying against the seat back ... he must get out, he must help. The door will not open. He kicks to no avail. Suddenly it flies open and there stands Vern in the shadow of a teetering roof beam, holding the door in his fists, his eyes as wide as saucers. A crying little girl stands beside him. Frank nearly falls from the cab. As Vern rushes towards him, flames leap up in a searing ball from the mangled vehicle and its shattered resting place. Irene sits in the driveway behind them, screaming.

"What do we do?" Vern shouts.

The older man does not answer; he steps out, turns to the cab, and, wincing from his wounds, begins hauling out the rifles. "This! I'm making my stand right here! You gonna stand with me?"

Standing dead still amidst the inferno, Vern stares, the thrown rifles falling uncaught beside him. In a split second, his mind seems to run forward in time, seconds, minutes ... he imagines the rows of police cars lining the street, lights flashing, guns aimed across the hoods, the somber blast of megaphones. And he pictures the ending. Just what Frank has been looking forward to — a deafening roar, a wall of lead puncturing the house like aluminum foil. And their dead bodies. Every one of them — his body, his son's, his daughter's. Cameras playing over their faces, lined up here stiff on the grass, the earnest voices of correspondents leading off the network news with muttered soundbites about the "culture wars turning deadly" into the glare of camera lights.

He is shaking his head "no" before the thought has even struck.

"Frank ..."

He is interrupted by the ear-filling wail of a siren and then, from behind them on the street, the squealing of tires.

He turns to see the blurred shape of a police car sliding to a stop, its passenger door already swinging open. There's no choice. He must retreat back through the house and try to escape from the backyard. Running with Heather in his arms back through the careening hallway, he hears Frank's first gunshots, a savage series of blasts that roar like a pounding across his chest.

At a later stage of the campaign for gay rights ... it will be time to get tough with remaining opponents. To be blunt, they must be vilified.

Marshall Kirk and Erastes Pill,
"The Overhauling of Straight America,"
Guide Magazine, November 1987.

EIGHTEEN

Her life comes to a halt with the ringing of the telephone. A woman's voice speaks. The reporter again.

"Gail, do you have any comment?"

"Comment on what?"

Gail hears the faint whine of the telephone wires for a long, tense moment. On the other end, Cari coughs hard, twice. "Well, uh, I have bad news for you. There was an attack on the house of Heather's foster family. A shoot-out with police. And the house burned to the ground. It looks like there're bodies inside. They haven't been identified yet, but ... Gail? Gail?"

Three miles away, in the newsroom of the *Boulder Daily Telegraph,* Cari hears a noise through her earpiece that turns her blood cold. The howling cry sounds barely human.

The press room bristles with the sound of journalism: camera shutters clicking, the faint hum of electricity, the creak of 150 people sitting anxiously on folding chairs. When the door opens and the two men step out, the noise explodes into a roar.

The Governor of Colorado and the State Patrol Chief sit down at a low table and cross their hands before them.

"I would like to begin," states the patrol chief, a Hispanic man in his late thirties. "In response to yesterday's firebombing and shoot-out at the home of a registered state foster parent, we have asked federal authorities to step in and investigate the presence in Colorado of a militant, armed group of religious fundamentalists. We have reason to believe, as many of you know, that a statewide network consisting of local churches and private individuals has been involved in helping criminal fugitives evade justice."

He looks up from his prepared sheet now, faces the cameras directly. "This is an extraordinary development because unlike previous civilian revolts, this conspiracy involves perhaps thousands of pastors and laypeople, almost exclusively of the Protestant Christian persuasion, who defy the normal labels of past extremist groups. These are seemingly normal, neighborhood churches who have placed themselves outside the law."

Cari Miner sits transfixed, scribbling hard on her pad. The pathetic Christian woman may have handed her the story of a lifetime. Her next move is clear. She absolutely must get a follow-up from Gail. Her boss might not like her disobeying orders, but not if she scoops every paper in Colorado on the widow's reaction ... She barely hears the governor speak in his ponderous, affected voice. "My fellow Coloradans, we must have the courage to expose and punish this extremist threat to our public safety ... "

The first thing Pastor Johnson notices is the ring of women surrounding her. Intensive care's fluorescent lights bathe the bed in a glow of ethereal whiteness, but the visitors seem to trace a dark perimeter around it, a shadowy orbit of black clothing and baleful expressions.

They turn as one at the sound of his footsteps. Under

their eyes he feels every layer of his alien status at once —
male, Christian, minister. Persona non grata.

Then, walking forward, he notices Sonya's face. He
barely recognizes the smooth battle mask of the woman
who confronted him hardly a week ago. The surface dam-
age strikes him first: the deep bruise staining her skin, the
shattered cheekbone, the intricate network of cuts and
scrapes across the right side of her face. Then something
about the eyes occurs to him. The glints of anger and
strength and pure aggression he remembers radiating there
have disappeared. It's as if someone opened a spigot and
allowed all the life to drain from them, leaving behind two
scorched holes which betray nothing but empty space.

"Sonya, I don't know if you remember me."

The voice comes soft and breathy, with only a thread of
the voice he remembers woven in. "Yeah, I do. What do
you want, *Pastor?*" She waits a second, draws a deep breath
and continues. "Come to preach to me in my hour of weakness?"

"No. I haven't come to preach."

"Why don't you save it for your flock," one of the lesbians tells him, her voice full and low after Sonya's delicate
whisper.

"Let's get back to your quilt square," says another girl,
barely eighteen, her back still turned to him.

He stands his ground. "I'd like to tell you something
very quickly, and then I'll leave. Can I do that?"

No. She cannot listen to this man. She can't afford to.
She has too much invested, too much at stake, to start letting this man's poison seep into her. So it shocks Sonya to
hear her own mouth tell him, sounding strangely vulner-
able, "Okay. Say it. But I warn you. One word of preaching
and I'll call security."

Despite her weakness Pastor Dave can feel the woman's
gaze on him, mixed in with vague surprise at his arrival
and a genuine curiosity at the nature of his errand. "Deal."

He moves closer to the bed, emboldened now by the pact

between them. He looks around at the brooding circle of women. "You can all hear this. I'm going to say this by way of personal example." He takes a deep breath and locks on to her eyes. "See, my dad is an alcoholic. I can honestly say, on account of the pain it's caused our family, that I hate alcoholism with a passion. But that doesn't mean I don't love my father. I do, and he knows it. I love him even though sometimes, in the middle of a binge, he'll start shouting that what we're seeing is actually his true self — that me and my mother and sister are the ones with the problem for wanting him sober. And every once in a while, he'll wake up from one of those binges just craving freedom from his life-style. He'll cry out to me for help. And every time he does, I'm there. That's what I want to tell you. I have a feeling you're starting to realize what a bill of goods you've been sold. Because you can have freedom. And when you're ready to ask for help, these people won't be there for you. But I will. I'll be there."

He pauses, feeling their hostile silence. His audacity seems to have left them speechless. Several of the women look to Sonya for their cue to react, but she remains fixed on him.

"Here's my card," he says. It's already in his hand, has been all along, gathering sweat. He holds it forward. Sonya does not take it. He lays it gently upon her blanket, over her stomach. The glares of her companions have reached white-hot intensity.

"Good-bye," he says, backing away to leave. "Remember that I care about you. Jesus cares about you. You can call me anytime."

He turns away with a half-smile, but a chorus of snickers beckons him to turn around, just in time to see Sonya's upraised fist crumple his card and toss it into a corner of the room.

"Don't hold your breath, preacher," comes her voice.

He exits to an explosion of laughter.

When the nurse returns on rounds, Sonya's friends have left — gone to sew together a five-foot square of fabric that will sum up her life.

In the silence of this room, she cannot escape the overwhelming sadness of knowing her whole existence will be reduced to a collage of symbolic images, quick-reference icons supposed to evoke the totality of who she was. Is that all her time on earth was about, she wonders? Protests, parades, political action, angry campaigning ... Why did her lesbianism have to become the single defining token of her time on earth? What has she accomplished with her life?

In these quiet moments the blinding pain returns, her constant companion since the accident. And worse still, the doubts return as well. Here, knowing AIDS may never allow her to leave this place, the old explanations and quick rationales ring hollow. "Internalized homophobia," the old gay rationale, is no longer wide enough to patch over the deep ache in her heart.

"Carol," she says weakly to the nurse beside her, "could you pick up that little ball, there in the corner, and hand it to me?"

There it is again. In the corner of her eye, a startling mirage stares at Gail from the backyard, just beyond the laundry room window. That beloved face, so near, smiling so sweetly ...

Her husband.

She rests her eyes on the trash bag in her hands, afraid to look again. By now, a day after the very first of these apparitions, she is not only shaken by the sight itself, but also by the terror of losing her sanity. Why is her mind playing with her so cruelly? The image of Vern seemed so real just now; the shadows of the old pine tree playing across his face, that shy grin he only wore when he was nervous, that tiny lock of hair falling down across his forehead ...

Then it in a blaze of clarity, it hits her: that was no illusion. The image was too real. Vern really is out there, waiting for her. She isn't crazy after all! She turns back to the window. And just as the three times before, the image has disappeared. Nothing but empty backyard. She feels the cruelty of it rip a hole through her spirit. Why did she have to believe so readily? Chiding herself for being such a fool, she blinks the tears away and bends down to finish tying the bag.

Nearing the policeman outside Gail's door, Cari walks with her very best casual saunter, relaxing her face into that smirk of easy familiarity reporters use to strike up a rapport with potential sources.

"How's Gail today?"

He shrugs. "Pretty rough. How would you feel if you thought your whole family was dead, and you had to wait for autopsies to know for sure?"

"You know, the thing is, officer — I'm hearing all these rumors. I'm hearing maybe there weren't as many bodies in that foster home as the media's reporting. Maybe only one. And they're not sure whose body it is. But no one will confirm. Nobody'll go off-record, even, so I'm stuck. I mean, what's going on?"

"I can't tell you; you know that."

"Come on. I've been here to talk to Gail, I've put in the time with her. You know I deserve a clue."

The man thinks a second, staring just beyond her head. He looks at her again, his eyes filled with disdain. "Hypotheticals. That's all I'm saying to you. If an autopsy on a badly burned body that finished up any minute from now, concluded that Vern Yates was still alive, where do you think the police would have the best chance of arresting him?"

For a second Cari feels very stupid. The officer smirks ever so slightly.

"Right here, within a half-mile of this house. He would have spent the last day or so near his wife, watching, waiting for just the right moment to come in and get her. Least, that's what I'd do."

"So what you're saying is ..."

"If I were a betting man, I wouldn't bet on Vern Yates being alive. Who else would try to kidnap his daughter from a foster home? That body has got to be him. But if it's not, then twenty minutes after the autopsy this place will be crawling with surveillance and he'll be caught for sure. And you wouldn't have a chance in the world of getting in to interview Gail. So you might want to hurry. Just in case." She turns towards the door and he taps her on the shoulder. "Oh, and one other thing."

"What's that?"

"When you talk to Gail, you keep your rumors to yourself."

The face peering through Gail's front door crack is less confident this time; the eyes wide and pleading.

"Please — can I talk to you? I'll just take a minute."

Without a word Gail just backs up from the open door, turns away and walks back to the living room. Cari follows a bit sheepishly. In a corner of the kitchen, two matronly women standing over a table covered with casseroles and covered dishes, cast chilly stares her way. *Church friends*, Cari thinks, amused at how quickly their demeanor gives them away.

"Gail, honey? You don't have to do this," calls out one of the kitchen friends.

Cari glares back at the women, realizing that as long as they are in the same room with her, the interview will not proceed. "Would it be easier if we stepped outside? Just a walk ..."

Without answering, Gail stands slowly and returns to

the front door. She opens and calls out to the dark-shirted figure standing guard a few feet away. "Officer, you know that park you let me walk to sometimes?" He nods respectfully. "Would you mind if this reporter and I went there for an interview?"

"It'll be the last time. I'll have to go with you ..."

"That's fine."

On an early spring evening, Boulder is a beautiful place. The Flatirons and their surrounding mountains raise an abrupt grey backdrop, their ragged silhouette framing a sky ablaze with ochre and turquoise.

Trailed quietly by the policeman, Gail walks beside the reporter, looking down at the grass. "What do you want me to tell you? You want me to tell you I'm in pain? Is this going to be a surprise for your readers?"

"No. I want to hear the truth."

"Do you really? Will they let you print it?"

Cari sighs deeply. "Yeah. They will. You nailed me with your challenge, you know. I found out there are liars and bigots in places I'd never dreamed of. I can't get this issue straight anymore. And I bet a lot of readers feel the same way."

They reach the park as Gail gathers her thoughts. She sits on a white bench on the lawn's edge. At the other end, an athletically built man throws a frisbee to a black Labrador. A toddler stands beside him, watching, clapping his hands clumsily. Gail looks away, glancing towards the policeman who has discreetly installed himself near the street, watching the flamboyant sunset.

She looks down again. She shakes her head, frustrated by her inability to clear her mind. "Listen. I don't think this is going to work. I'm still ... in shock."

"I know. I just thought it might help to talk it out."

"There's a time for talking things out, Cari. And this isn't it. There was a time for prayer, before yesterday. And now, it's gone too." Gail looks down at the grass, and embarrassment creeps into her voice. "Right now, I'm just fighting to keep from going crazy. My mind's starting to play tricks on me. For the last couple of days, I've thought I've seen members of my family through the window. Vern, John, even Heather once. Just standing in a bush, or behind a tree, looking at me, smiling. And of course when I look back again, they're gone. It's agonizing."

"Yeah, but it's natural. A lot of people I've talked to see their loved ones after a tragedy. Has all this affected your faith?"

"Some. God and I aren't really on speaking terms right now. Actually, we're on shouting terms. You know something? After pounding the walls and yelling at Him to show His face, I used to sit for awhile and get quiet, and sometimes get the deepest, most peaceful confidence that He heard me. That my family was in His hands. I don't feel that anymore."

"Have you actually stopped believing in God?"

Desperately biting her lower lip, Gail looks around aimlessly, as if the motion will brush away the tears. "No, I don't think so. I'm just through asking Him for anything right now."

The policeman walks across the grass toward the frisbee thrower.

"You know, when you're a believer, there's times when that awful little thought runs through your head: what if my faith is in vain? What if there is no God, and everything I feel is just self-deception? And then other times, God just feels so close that denying His existence would be like denying the hair on your head."

She rubs her face, hard, the fingers leaving pale marks across her cheeks. "Right now I feel nothing. Neither one. If anything, I feel indifferent. Maybe I believed too much in America — God and Country. But America's let me down, so maybe right now I'm blaming God for something that's the nation's fault. I don't know ... " She looks away, into the sunset. "If God doesn't want me to have my family back, then it's up to Him to tell me His plans. I begged, I pleaded for Him to reveal Himself to me. To show me some sign. A sign that He cares, a sign of anything ... "

Then she sees it again. Her eyes focus desperately. A figure. Standing at the end of a small passage between the bushes. A boy, barely visible in the waning light.

Her boy.

To Cari it seems this woman is starting to lose it — staring off into the bushes, furrowing her eyebrows and twisting her whole face into a contorted mixture of surprise and disbelief.

Gail keeps staring, then blinks rapidly several times. Her eyes are deceiving her again. She looks down again, away from the sight, and her shoulders start to shake from sobs too deep for sound.

Then she looks up again.

It's real. Her Johnny is still there, watching her patiently, beckoning with his hand.

She feels a sudden rush of calm overwhelm her, like a clear wave of fresh water. She turns to her interviewer with a smile that Cari will forever swear looked like the serenity of someone gone completely insane.

"Would you like to leave?" Cari asks.

"No," Gail answers. "It's okay. I'm okay. I'd just like to ... walk by myself for a bit."

She stands and begins walking in a straight line, tracing an odd beeline for the bushes. Cari is still too dumbstruck at her behavior to speak, but she turns toward the policeman and he has seen it too, watching intently from his spot a hundred yards away.

Gail turns back, smiling broadly now.

"I'll be all right. Don't worry."

She breaks into a run. The last image of her which Cari remembers is the sight of Gail running, her hand going to her mouth.

She hears a cry, muffled. Only then, in a belated rush of good sense, does Cari squint hard for a good look through the branches. And there she can almost make out the figure of a boy, running toward Gail.

Across the park, the policeman shouts and begins sprinting towards them, fumbling with his holster. He pulls the gun and yells "Stop!" at the top of his lungs, hurdles a small wooden fence, runs across the last strip of grass and breaks through a last line of branches.

Then he is the one who stops.

Before him, in a small clearing in the bushes, stand a young boy and a grown man and Gail and a very young girl. They stand together, holding each other so close, so tightly, that they appear as a single clump of humanity.

The officer's mind, filled a second ago with the clamoring rush of adrenaline, now only knows the overwhelming power of this picture, of the children's arms reaching around their parents' legs and the joy in Gail's tear-filled eyes. He wants to shout out the usual warnings, but his mouth will not work. He stammers a few syllables. He feels almost ashamed for the gun in his hand. The father's eyes reach out to him, pleading. *How can you break up such a family?*

Finally, words come to him.

"Go. Go! *GO!!*"

They begin running away, the father flashing a brief, grateful smile. Just then Cari Miner arrives alongside and glances quickly at his frozen pose, then at the fleeing figures disappearing through another clump of bushes. Neither one moves. At the same instant they both become aware of a squealing sound approaching them from the street.

Through the outer veil of branches the officer sees a van speed by, then hears a violent screeching of tires on pavement and the sound of a side door being rolled open. A door slams abruptly and tires screech again.

The Yates are gone.

I think the time for violence has arrived. I don't personally think I'm the guy with the guts to do it, but I'd like to see an AIDS terrorist army.

Larry Kramer, founder of the extremist group ACT-UP and one of the "elder statesmen" of the homosexual movement.

We shall be victorious because we are fueled with the ferocious bitterness of the oppressed who have been forced to play seemingly bit parts in your dumb, heterosexual shows throughout the ages. We too are capable of firing guns and manning the barricades of the ultimate revolution.

Gay activist Michael Swift,
"Towards a Homoerotic Order," 1987.

NINETEEN

Letter from a fugitive

Cari Miner
A Conservative Times exclusive

BOULDER – I must admit, I never thought my name would appear above an article in what my old employers, the *Boulder Daily Telegraph,* always called a "Radical Right Rag."

But, then again, my old employers would never have published this story. I know, because turning in this story cost me my job. And, to my amazement, I find that this is the only place where I can actually tell the truth.

You see, one of the most baffling and challenging stories of my career ended recently. With a letter.

As the state police have duly noted, it is a letter delivered without a postmark.

It is a letter filled with the mystery and wonder of a distraught mother who, sitting beside me less than two weeks ago, cried out to her God for a sign — and then, by all appearances, received it.

It is a letter written by a woman who pondered aloud, before me, the possibility of her God being cruel and heartless. Then, within minutes, she was gone, spirited away by the apparent answer to her prayers.

The letter I received came in a plain white envelope, addressed in a hand different from the writer of the letter inside. It closes out, at least for the moment, a news story which was followed throughout Colorado, and even the nation, with great interest and controversy.

The letter's author was Gail Yates.

You may have read the press reports that I was involved in the

183

escape and disappearance of Gail Yates from a Boulder park last week. Involved, that is, because it is I who requested that Gail be allowed, under police escort, to walk with me to a park for a quiet interview. I watched Gail walk away from the bench, disappear into a clump of willow trees, and then heard the getaway van pulling away at high speed. Police have not reconstructed the exact nature of her escape, but it appears that members of the so-called Network drove up and, with split-second timing, spirited her and her family away.

Some would say I was the accessory, however unwitting, to the escape of a convicted homophobe, a psychological child abuser, a defier of our state's educational codes. In retrospect — and I have had many hours now to reflect on my coverage of the Yates story — I have a hard time exhuming real instances of hatred or malice in Gail. I remember mostly pain, disillusionment, and a sense of real betrayal by a nation she had once considered amicable to her beliefs.

The days to follow would reveal that, contrary to sensationalistic reports in the press, only one person was killed in the attack on her daughter's foster home. And that person was in fact not her fugitive husband, or her son.

It is true that someone in the house fired on police officers with an automatic rifle. Yet, as the facts now show, that shooter, who died in the exchange of gunfire, was not Vern Yates, as universally reported. I have further learned that the fiery truck crash which set the tragedy in motion was not planned or carried out by Yates but caused instead by the reckless actions of a state police auxiliary.

Not only were Gail's loved ones alive during our last conversation, but they were nearby, waiting for the chance to show themselves and take her away with them into hiding.

Yet when I spoke to her none of this was known. It seemed highly likely that Gail's entire family was now lost to her — her daughter to the courts, her husband and son to bullets and fire.

It goes without saying that you won't read this in a mainstream newspaper. They're too busy milking the familiar stereotype of the "militant right-winger" to bother with the facts.

I have relearned an old, familiar lesson — a lesson we should all remember.

Don't believe everything you read.

Sadly, journalism today is not the reliable source it was when I was growing up, or studying it in college. Instead of a bastion of impartial truth, I find that my field has degenerated into little more than a tool for advancing pet doctrines and ideologies.

So don't settle for the broad headlines or the easy soundbites. The truth today demands harder work, deeper digging.

In that spirit of truth, I have decided after much thought that although my letter from Gail is personal, I will reproduce it here.

Dear Cari,

My memories of the joyous, wonderful reunion I have had with my family are mixed in somehow with the image of your eyes, questioning and surprised as I stood up from that park bench. I have hugged my husband and my children so many times since then, their shoulders must be getting sore. But my children don't complain. Like me, they didn't think we'd ever be together again. Yet, burdened with the desire to share my heart with you, I write today from the road, where we will remain until America returns to her senses.

As you might imagine, Vernon and John and Heather and I are far away from Boulder right now. As for how this letter has reached you without postage, let me just say that you have no idea how many people across this nation

share our concern and our outrage at the treatment of conservative Christians these days.

But that's not why I'm writing.

I'm writing because I have not forgotten the questioning look in your eyes during the last moments of our final interview, as I vented the doubts and anguish I was going through. Now, having spent many hours hugging and kissing my children who have been restored to me, I can tell you that God does answer prayer.

I regret my weakness, in those last moments before I walked away. Just at the moment when I deserved it least, when I most doubted the sovereignty of the living God, He saw fit to grant my request. So I tell you, Cari, quite personally, that the God I worship is quite able to see me through any trial. He is bigger than the government, bigger than the NEA, bigger than the police.

He is capable, even, of healing this country I love, despite the incredible hatred and hypocrisy which has it in a stranglehold today.

Where there is God, there is hope, Cari. Always hope.

Love in Christ,
Gail Yates

◆ ◆ ◆

Looks like you did it, God. I don't quite know how, but then again, knowing how isn't my job. All I know is, my family's back together again, and I didn't think it was possible. Thanks. I promise I'll appreciate them more than I did all these years.

Now it seems the next part is up to me. I look back now, and it's so clear what a shallow life I used to lead. And it's so clear you've taken me to something different. I wasn't asking for it, but you pulled me up to a whole new level of commitment. I'm not sure what it means, or where it will lead. But one thing I know for sure; I'll tackle it with every ounce of strength you give me. I'm not gonna look the other way. I'm not gonna run from the challenge.

Thanks for leading me here. Thanks for yanking me out of my complacent life into this thrilling, terrifying adventure. Thank you, Jesus. It's a hard place to be, but if this is where you want us, I wouldn't want to be anywhere else.

The brand new refugees have followed their instructions to the letter: bought an old station wagon for cash from a used car lot on the seedy side of town, driven it sputtering up Interstate 70 into the northern mountains for an hour and a half, kept to the speed limit, watched for pursuers and police. They've pulled over at a rest stop, raised the hood as if broken down, and stepped out. The three young daughters have stood tensely against their mother's legs, silently clutching her downstretched fingers. They've anxiously watched every car that drove past. They've waited.

They do not notice the mountain biker stopped in the brush far above them. Even had they managed to spot his distant form, they would not be able to discern the thin mouthpiece curving from his helmet, or the odd bulk of the scope he holds before his eyes, scanning the small valley surrounding them. They would not see his lips moving, speaking carefully coded descriptions of the area's security status. They could not see the command vehicle parked beside a stream four miles away, or, inside, the banks of electronic consoles receiving the bicyclist's message, or hear the soft voices of people relaying another message to a transport team.

At precisely ten o'clock, a nondescript passenger van pulls up beside them and stops abruptly. A brown-haired man in the passenger seat smiles warmly, lowers his window, and calls out in a reassuring voice. "You folks look like a bunch of Refugees!"

A great peal of stored-up laughter erupts from the whole family. Belatedly, the husband remembers his prearranged reply. "You got that right, brother."

The man jumps out and moves quickly to grab a suitcase. "Patrick," the husband says tentatively, offering his hand.

His rescuer answers with a firm shake and a deep, confident gaze that warms Patrick to the core. "The name's Vern. Vern Yates. Welcome to the Network. Your days of running alone are over."

AFTERWORD

If the preceding strikes you as a story of unbelievable madness, few people would disagree with you. That does not mean, however, that these events are not possible — even likely. Especially if we remain silent, and continue to give up our voice in the culture.

In fact, many of these things have already taken place — as the brief descriptions preceding each chapter clearly indicate. Attempts to make "homophobia" a mental illness are in progress. So are on-the-job "sensitivity training" sessions, where employees unwilling to personally embrace homosexuality are intimidated and threatened with firing. And schoolhouse indoctrination into the merits of "sexual diversity" is taking place across America.

If all you've heard for the past few years is the liberal media's take on "gay rights," this story may strike you as new and unheard of. You may have accepted the doctored image of oppressed, powerless gay outcasts fighting for their basic freedoms.

If so, I ask you to check out the facts. Look at what has already occurred. Discover how the leaders of the gay movement actually describe their goals behind closed doors, outside of camera range.

The plot of *Refuge* is directly based on the realization of three very real trends active in America today. Three trends which, if unopposed, could very easily and quickly lead to a complete loss of rights on the part of those who hold traditional values.

Trend 1: the attempt to impose "multicultural" school curricula on every schoolchild in America. The educational establishment in this country is dedicated to imposing initiatives like "Project 10" and the "Rainbow Curriculum" on all American schoolchildren. They include a complete affirmation of homosexuality, indoctrination into "safe sex" and denunciation of all "homophobic" opposition to homosexuality — starting at the kindergarten level. Already, states like Minnesota have changed their child-abuse statutes to include "failure to provide necessary education" as grounds for neglect charges. In New York state, parents have had their children forcibly removed for such "crimes" as breast-feeding and spanking. (New York *Freedom's Alert*, Aug. 1993, p. 4)

Trend 2: *the movement, led by the United Nations Convention on the Rights of the Child, to declare children "autonomous" and "sovereign," and designate the state as the final judge of the child's best physical, moral and spiritual interests — leaving the parents few, if any, legal rights.* Already, nations who've adopted this measure have witnessed scenarios frighteningly similar to those in *Refuge* — including the aforementioned raid by French police against seven Christian families.

The bottom line: under the U.N. Convention the government determines children's welfare, and these parents' beliefs run afoul of state policy. Meanwhile, the current presidential administration enthusiastically endorses U.S. ratification of this same Convention.

Trend 3: *the movement to have "homophobia," (i.e., any disapproval whatsoever of homosexuality) declared an official, legally recognized mental illness.* Hard as it may be to believe, there is an organized campaign to have "homophobia" declared a mental illness — even to have it included in the American Psychiatric Association's DSM-III, the official register of mental illnesses (from which homosexuality was removed with great fanfare in 1973). In the spring of 1993, homosexual physicians held a high-level meeting with Health and Human Services Secretary Donna Shalala, which included discussion of declaring "anti-gay bigotry" to be a "national health hazard." It's an almost laughable proposition, but it's proceeding nonetheless. As you might imagine, being declared "mentally ill" carries severe legal ramifications — especially for parents.

To those of us following these trends, the picture of America shown by *Refuge* seems entirely possible — if her citizens don't stand up and contend for their rights. The only way to protect our future is to think about it in the present.

Remember also, that those who oppose homosexual extremism do not condone, or even tolerate, actual harassment or mistreatment of those who disagree with them. This is not about encouraging "gay bashing" in any form whatsoever. It is about preserving the right to disagree with and oppose, in a civil and compassionate manner, the forced affirmation of the homosexual life-style.

So, please get involved. Let's keep this book a work of fiction. Let's keep it from becoming an awful prophecy of life to come in America.

APPENDIX

DOCUMENTATION OF QUOTES

Chapter 1

"... now the tide has turned. We have at last 'come out,' and in doing so have exposed the mean-spirited nature of Judeo-Christian morality ... But with the help of a growing number of your own membership, we are going to force you to recant everything you have believed or said about sexuality ... If all of these things do not come to pass quickly, we will subject Orthodox Jews and Christians to the most sustained hatred and vilification in recent memory. We have captured the liberal establishment and the press. We have already beaten you on a number of battlefields. And we have the spirit of the age on our side. You have neither the faith nor the strength to fight us, so you might as well surrender now."
— Steve Warren, "Warning to the Homophobes," *The Advocate,* 1 September 1987, p. 29.

Chapter 2

"The family unit — spawning ground of lies, betrayals, mediocrity, hypocrisy and violence — will be abolished.The family unit, which only dampens imagination and curbs free will, must be eliminated."
— Michael Swift, "Towards a Homoerotic Order," *Gay Community News,* 7 November 1987.

Chapter 3

"Boy lovers and the lesbians who have young lovers ... are not child molesters. The child abusers are priests, teachers, therapists, cops and parents who force their staid morality onto the young people in their custody."
— Pat Califia's essay, "Man/Boy Love and the Lesbian/Gay Movement," *The Age Taboo: Gay Male Sexuality, Power and Consent* (Boston and London: Alyson Publications/Gay Men's Press, 1981), p. 144.

Chapter 4

"All churches who oppose us will be closed. Our only gods are handsome young men ..."
— Michael Swift, "Towards a Homoerotic Order," *Gay Community News,* 7 November 1987.

"The rioters assumed complete control of the exterior property and grounds of the church... . The guest speaker was escorted by police to the church as debris from the rioters pelted him from all sides... . When the rioters saw children standing in the lobby, they shouted, 'We want your children! Give us your children!' ... A nine-year-old boy was crying in hysterics. 'They are after me. It's me they want.' He did not calm down until the family was several miles from the building."
— Excerpts from the official report of Pastor David Innes of Hamilton Square Baptist Church, San Francisco, following the September 19, 1993 mob attack by several hundred members of ACT-UP, Queer Nation, and Lesbian Avengers.

Chapter 5

1991. Mandatory "sensitivity training" lectures are held at a state hospital in Pueblo, Colorado. Employees are urged to sign a form acknowledging their "imperfect attitudes toward gays and lesbians" and to wear buttons stating, "it's okay to be gay." Those who decline are walked to the front, told to turn and face their colleagues.
— From the document, "Training sexual orientation," State of Colorado Department of Institutions, 1991 and corroborated by first hand accounts given to Colorado For Family Values.

1994. George Mason University punishes as "discrimination" the act of "jumping when a homosexual touches you on the arm," and "keeping a physical distance from someone because they are a known gay or lesbian."
— Charles Colson, "Postmodern Power Grab," *Christianity Today,* 20 June 1994, p. 80.

Chapter 6

"... demanding a separation between church and state isn't enough; the churches' basic doctrines must be changed, with homophobia written out forever."
— Michelangelo Signorile, "Throw the Book at Them," *Out,* November 1994, p. 32.

1994. A Mississippi gay man files suit in federal court against the Oxford University Press demanding both $45 million in damages and the immediate deletion of all scripture verses describing homosexuality as sinful. "The Bible abused and oppressed me," claims Ford, "when it said homosexuality is a sin, because I was born a homosexual."
— "Man suing Bible publishers for discrimination," *San Francisco Sentinel,* 5 October 1994, p. 12.

Chapter 7

1993. After signing the U.N. Covenant on the Rights of the Child, the French government raids seven Christian homes, separating children from their parents, searching property, confiscating documents, arresting adults. Children are interrogated for up to ten hours and permanently placed in a state reeducation center. Because they home school, teach religion and occasionally spank, two mothers are imprisoned for five weeks. Parents are denied contact with their children. Parents are told their children wish no communication with them.
— "French Government Raids Christian Homes," *Colorado Christian News,* August 1993, p. 16.

1995. A Washington journalist sponsors an initiative which would prevent Washington state agencies from placing children in the custody of anyone "who practices right-wing fundamentalist Christianity."
— "Striking back: Anti-fundamentalist initiative filed," *OutNOW!,* 13 June 1995, p. 1.

Chapter 8

1992. The Denver Post reports Denver public school teachers face pressure to teach homosexuality is normal, beginning in kindergarten.
— *The Denver Post,* 2 December, 1990, p. 1.

"Is it possible your heterosexuality is just a phase you may outgrow? How can you hope to become a whole person if you ... remain unwilling to explore and develop your normal, natural, healthy, homosexual potential?"
– Question # 14 contained in "Gay and Lesbian Youth Tools for Educators," a teacher's guide distributed by the Denver Public Schools' Health and Science Education Department, 1992.

The questionnaire, presented to teachers by gay instructors during a taxpayer-funded continuing education course, states bluntly: "There is no biblical sex ethic. The Bible knows only a love ethic, which is constantly being brought to bear on whatever sexual mores are dominant in a given country, culture or period."
The questionnaire, designed to be answered by heterosexual high school students, asked other questions, including:

"5. Is it possible that all you need is a good gay lover?

7. If you have never slept with a person of the same sex, how do

you know that you would not prefer to do so?

12. The majority of child molesters are heterosexuals. Do you really consider it safe to expose children to heterosexual teachers?

14. How can you hope to become a whole person if you limit yourself to an exclusive heterosexual object choice and remain unwilling to explore and develop your normal, natural, healthy homosexual potential?

19. How could the human race survive if everyone were heterosexual like you, considering the menace of overpopulation?"

In addition to aggressively promoting acceptance of homosexuality, bisexuality, lesbianism, and condom use (with graphic descriptions of these behaviors and techniques), this teachers' guide urged teachers to give children pamphlets containing telephone numbers of possible adult gay mentors.

Chapter 9

"Some people may need professional help to deal with their phobia of gay or lesbian people, just as some need help to deal with fear of heights or elevators."
– Pamphlet entitled, *Homophobia: What Are We So Afraid Of?* distributed in schools by the Lesbian and Gay Public Awareness Project, compliments of National Coming Out Day, 1993.

Chapter 10

"... businesses will fail, people will be fired for feelings or beliefs about homosexuality, because homosexuals will claim persecution and discrimination. Your freedom of speech will be violated. These are all costly enough as it is. But your children, your grandchildren, they will be taught the 'virtues of homosexual lifestyles.' They will be counseled further into mental illness and untold thousands will die ..."
– Jeff (a pseudonym), "A Warning to Heterosexuals," personal letter, 1993.

Chapter 11

1989. Homosexuals invade mass at New York City's St. Patrick's Cathedral, shouting obscenities, throwing condoms, and defiling Communion elements.

1991. A Minneapolis Catholic Archdiocese is fined $15,000 and assessed $20,000 in damages after homosexuals complain the church denied them their "right" to meet in church-owned facilities.

1991. Gay demonstrators dressed in suits and ties infiltrate a brunch at First Baptist Church of Atlanta, then suddenly pepper the diners with hundreds of condoms, and chant,"safer sex saves lives!"
— "AIDS activists crash church brunch," *Atlanta Journal Constitution,* 17 November, 1991.

1992. The Attorney General of Hawaii rules that, under a state "gay rights" law, church leaders are legally required to consider homosexuals for all church positions except the pastorate itself.

1992. A New Jersey "gay rights" law prohibits all employers, including churches, from discriminating on the basis of "sexual orientation," and requires churches to marry homosexuals.
— National Association of Evangelicals' *Washington Insight,* July, 1992.

1994. In Sweden, an evangelical pastor is jailed for preaching a sermon from Romans 1 ruled to be "belittling" to homosexuals.
— Roger Magnuson, *Informed Answers to Gay-Rights Questions,* (Portland, Oregon: Multnomah Press, 1994), p. 55.

Chapter 12

"I have helped to create a truly fascist organization ... We conspired to bring into existence an activist group that ... could effectively exploit the media for its own ends, and would work covertly and break the law with impunity ... we subscribed to consciously subversive modes, drawn largely from the voluminous Mein Kampf, which some of us studied as a working model. As ACT-UP/D.C. grew, we struck intently and surgically into whatever institution we believed to stand in our way ... "
— Eric Pollard, "First Things," *Washington Blade,* 31 January 1991.

Chapter 13

"I think the time for violence has arrived. I don't personally think I'm the guy with the guts to do it, but I'd like to see an AIDS terrorist army."
— Larry Kramer, ACT-UP founder, quoted in *Wall Street Journal,* 8 May 1990.

"We shall be victorious because we are fueled with the ferocious bitterness of the oppressed who have been forced to play seemingly bit parts in your dumb, heterosexual shows throughout the ages. We too are capable of firing guns and manning the barricades of the

ultimate revolution."
— Michael Swift, "Towards a Homoerotic Order," *Gay Community News,* 7 November 1987.

Chapter 14

1989. Anne Ready and Maureen Rowe of Madison, Wisconsin advertise for a third roommate. When a lesbian answers, Ann replies, "No thanks." The lesbian files a discrimination complaint.

Ann and Maureen are summoned before Madison's Equal Opportunity Commission. They are interrogated for hours, ordered to pay thousands in damages, to write a letter of apology, to have their rental decisions monitored for the next two years, and to attend "sensitivity training" at a local homosexual organization. The commission rules that their personal objections to homosexuality are invalid. Pleading that this would bankrupt them, they are told, "That's not our problem." The commission rules they lost their right to privacy when they entered the public marketplace.

1992. After three years, enormous public outcry and a $10,000 legal tab, the Madison City Council drops the penalties.
— Katharine Dalton, "Privacy and the 'Lesbian Roommate' Case," *Wall Street Journal,* 20 July 1992.

Chapter 15

"... [homosexuals] possess political power much greater than their numbers ... they devote this political power to achieving not merely a grudging social toleration, but full societal acceptance, of homosexuality."
— Justice Antonin Scalia, dissenting opinion, Evans v. Romer, United States Supreme Court decision, 20 May 1996, p. 11.

"By the year 2000, it will be impossible to get agreement, anywhere in the civilized world, that it is not OK to be lesbian or gay."
— Advertisement in *San Francisco Sentinel,* 19 May 1993, p. 6.

Chapter 16

" ... concensus grows among mental health professionals that homophobia, the irrational fear and hatred of homosexuals, is a psychological abnormality that interferes with the judgment and reliability of those afflicted."
— Dr. Richard Isay, Letter to the editor, *New York Times,* 2 September 1992.

Chapter 17

1984. The Seattle City Council considers an ordinance making it a crime to "discredit, demoralize, or belittle another person by words or conduct" based on sexual orientation.
— "Menacing gays could be made a crime," *Seattle Post-Intelligencer,* 11 May 1984.

1994. The government of Ontario, Canada, imposes a speech code law on its universities, banning comments about sexual orientation found to cause a "negative environment or climate." Students can file complaints if course work "hurt their feelings" or made them "uncomfortable." Speech overheard off-campus, at social functions, during academic work, even over the telephone, can be punished. Guilty students could be forced to apologize, suspended, ordered into "sensitivity training," even expelled.
— Jerry Carroll, "Political Correctness Takes a Nosedive," *San Francisco Chronicle,* 26 October 1994, p. E-7.

1995. A federal district court affirms a New Jersey "gay rights" amendment which makes it illegal to say or print anything which could indirectly "promote discrimination" against homosexuals.
— Press release, "Federal Court Rules that New Jersey Gay Rights Amendment Overrides Free Speech Claims," The Rutherford Institute.

Chapter 18

"At a later stage of the campaign for gay rights ... it will be time to get tough with remaining opponents. To be blunt, they must be vilified."
— Marshall Kirk and Erastes Pill, "The Overhauling of Straight America," *Guide Magazine,* November 1987.

Chapter 19

"You have to understand that the motivations of the gay community are validation. They want to be approved. They want people to say, 'It's okay that you're gay.' So basically the gay community is trying to turn the world into a 12-step gay support group, trying to get everyone out there to be a member ... and if you disagree with one tiny, insignificant little point of their wide, broad, sweeping agenda, you're all of a sudden a homophobe and a hatemonger. You're a villain. A bad guy. And this is ludicrous."
— Luke Montgomery, "Family News in Focus" radio broadcast, 21 June, 1995.

SPECIAL OFFER

Get the whole truth about Colorado's historic fight for Amendment 2 in the nonfiction book: *GAY POLITICS VS COLORADO and America: The Inside Story of Amendment 2*, by Stephen Bransford, ISBN 0-9639465-0-1 (cloth)

Regular price $22 hardback available at a special discount to the readers of *REFUGE,* only $15, shipping included. Send check or money order to:

Sardis Press
Box 11
Cascade CO 80809

For additional copies of *REFUGE*, order through your local bookstore, or send $9.95 plus $2 shipping and handling to Sardis Press, or to Liberty House Publishers, Box 10307, Lynchburg, VA 24506.